Being Amani

ANNABELLE STEELE

Published in Great Britain by Hashtag BLAK an imprint
of Hashtag Press 2021

A CIP catalogue for this book is available from the British Library.

ISBN 978-1-9138350-4-0

Typeset in Garamond Classic 11.25/14 by Blaze Typesetting

Printed and bound in Great Britain by Clays Ltd, Elcograf S.p.A.

HASHTAG BLAK
Hashtag Press Ltd
Kent, England, United Kingdom
www.hashtagblak.co.uk
Twitter: @hashtag_blak

Hashtag BLAK is an imprint of Hashtag Press Ltd
Website: www.hashtagpress.co.uk

This book is dedicated to every girl, every young woman and every Queen who has ever found herself looking for happiness in all the wrong places.

ACKNOWLEDGEMENTS

To the women. . .

There are so many women to thank, so many women who have believed in me and so many women who have encouraged me to keep going over the years. From teachers to friends to family members and colleagues, I am so incredibly lucky to be surrounded by such amazing women!

Of course, I would like to thank my mum for believing in me and inspiring me in everything that I do. For cheering me on and for encouraging me to follow my heart at all times. Through you I have learned to be strong and graceful. Through you I have learned to be me. You've taught me to always have faith, to look for the positives and to find the silver lining in every situation. I am forever grateful!

Thank you to *all* of my friends and family, with special thanks to these ladies: Cherelle Ekepe, Katy Burton, Tina Steele, Aunty Corine, Louise Rosario-Tulloch, Aunty Mel, Stephanie Woodworth, Sarah Brazier, Katie Neil, Faye Preston, Jess Heaney, Rachel Shaw, Rosie Hegarty, Janine Ojinnaka, Maryrose Ojinnaka, Daisy Pointing, Dionne Anderson, Chanel Spooner, Afiya Chocollo, Lucette Henderson and Yousra Imran for constantly reminding me that I am Queen in the presence of Queens! I would like to thank you all for continually talking me up! For the constant encouraging messages! For the support! For the pep talks and the kicks up the bum! Thank you for listening to me moan, for hyping me up and for all of your kind words! This one is for all of you! (Hopefully I haven't missed anyone.)

Thank you to Helen, Luisa and Abiola at Hashtag Blak for sharing Amani's story, for believing in me and for helping me see it through to the end. I am forever grateful for all of your patience and hard work! Thank you for creating Hashtag Blak and for being dedicated to sharing the stories of underrepresented voices. Thanks for just being the Boss Babes that you are!

I would like to thank everyone who has entertained Ezra while I have been planning, writing and editing. Without you all, it literally would not have been possible!

And finally. . . although this is about the women in my life, I would like to thank my husband for listening to me moan about everything and anything. For sitting with me and discussing plotlines until midnight (on more than one occasion). For getting excited about my writing when I had lost all faith. For not allowing me to give up when I wanted to throw the whole book away! Thank you for allowing me to follow my dreams and for holding my hand along the way. Eternally grateful!

THAT NIGHT

I lay in bed scrolling endlessly through Instagram and saving images of Black girls with big smiles and long, beautiful braids as inspiration for my next hairstyle. Nao's latest single plays on repeat in my earphones. My eyes feel heavy and I know that sleep will come soon.

I jolt up to the sound of smashing and crashing coming from downstairs. Without thinking, I look in the direction of my bedroom door. I pause the music, pull out my left earphone and freeze. I wait, hoping that it was just my imagination. I lean up on my forearm and tilt my head, as though it's going to help me hear better. I keep my eyes fixed on the door. The room is in complete darkness apart from the blue light coming from my phone, which is casting long shadows on the walls.

I realise I've been holding my breath and the bedsheets are sticking to my clammy body while I wait for the inevitable. Another smash, louder than the first, but this time I jolt so violently that my phone slips out of my hand and falls on the bed. My heart's racing and my body begins to shake. Most people would call the police and report that an intruder had entered their home, but I know it's not an intruder. I know that they live here and I know what's coming next.

I can't just sit and listen to them arguing again. I ball my hands into fists as my fingertips fizz and tingle with anger, but I'm rooted to the spot. The quilt shackles me to the bed.

Come on Amani, get up!

Nothing. I take a deep breath and exhale as I force the quilt of my body. I climb silently out of my bed and creep across the room towards the door, being careful not to step anywhere the floorboards creak.

I open my bedroom door, just a crack, and the light from the hallway floods my room. There's mumbling and another smash, but this time I don't jump. I'm numb. Their voices gets louder and clearer as they move into the hallway. The footsteps give away the exact location of my parents. I know this house well and I know that they are directly below my room.

I squeeze my lips together and close my eyes, praying that it stops me from crying. I shake my head in disbelief. I can't believe this is happening again.

A shrill scream pierces through the house and I immediately clasp my hands across my mouth. I want to run downstairs and see if Mum is okay, but I'm scared. Scared of making things worse, and of what I'll see, but mostly I'm scared that Dad will turn on me.

I glance at my wrist and wince, remembering the pain from the last time. It only happened once, but once was enough.

My heart races as the blood pumps around my ears. It's making it difficult for me to hear anything else. I take my hands off my mouth and hold on to the doorframe to steady myself.

Mum and Dad have argued a lot recently; it's got worse since she lost the baby but I thought things were finally looking up. They were fine this weekend, but Dad's been drinking tonight.

Is that what they're arguing about? Mum hates it when he drinks—we both do. He gets braver and meaner and more. . . well, more like this.

I creep out of my room to the top of the stairs and look up at the clock in the hallway. It's 2:13am. I wish I was still in bed, drifting off to sleep as Nao serenades me. My chest hurts and I finally exhale. I didn't realise I was holding my breath again. They're still shouting at each other. I crouch down on the top step and I just about make out some of their words.

"Kill."

"Trust."

"STOP!"

I use the back of my hand to wipe my eyes. When did I start crying?

The living room door swings open and ricochets against the wall with a loud bang. I jump back so that I'm definitely out of sight. I don't even know what I'm doing.

Mum runs along the hallway, her boots pounding on the wooden floorboards. I'm relieved when I see her. I feared she was slumped on the floor injured. She grabs a couple of bags from the hallway and violently yanks open the front door and storms out into the darkness. Where is she going?

I run back to my room and race over to the window. It's pouring with rain and the trees are blowing violently in the wind, casting spindly shadows all over the front garden. This is weird weather for the middle of July in London, and I can't help but think that the way I'm feeling is somehow affecting the weather tonight.

All the other houses on the street are in complete darkness. I can see Mum across the street putting the bags into the car and closing the boot. Is she packing his things or hers? She wouldn't leave without me, would she?

She frantically fights against the wind. She runs back towards the house and I sigh, relieved. I hear her coming up the stairs, her boots beating on the carpeted steps. She would never normally wear wet boots on the carpet. She speeds up and slows down, missing steps along the way.

Scared that she'll clock that I've been spying, I quickly jump back into bed and try to slow my breathing. I don't want her to know that the arguing woke me up. I push my earphones back into my ears, press play and wait.

Mum pushes open the door and quickly crosses the room to my bed. She kneels on the floor and holds my hand. Her touch instantly calms my breathing and although I'm still panicking, I feel slightly better having her here with me. She gently shakes me and pulls out my earphones.

"Amani, wake up. We have to go now," Mum whispers.

I slowly open my eyes pretending that I've just woke up. "Mum? What's going on?"

"Come on baby, just put these on." She hands me my beat-up, black and white, high-top Converse, khaki green trench and pair of joggers from the pile of clothes that I threw over the chair earlier.

I'm half expecting her to tell me that I need to clean my room as she looks around and grabs my phone charger and bag off the floor. I pull on the joggers over my pyjama shorts. This coat won't hold up against the unusual weather outside but I don't argue.

"The car's running. I've got your things," she says as she watches me zip up my coat.

I look around the room, filled with my stuff and wonder what 'things' she's got apart from the bag in her hand.

The light peeping in from the hallway allows me to just about make out her face—mascara is smeared across her cheeks. She looks exhausted and scared, a look I've seen many times. There's a blood-stained bandage wrapped around her wrist.

"Mum!" I point at her wrist. I immediately look down at my own wrist and grimace. Seeing her injured wrist instantly brings back the ache in my own arm.

I place my hand over her bandage and she looks away from me. For a moment we're still but then she sighs and pulls her wrist away out of sight.

What has happened? Where are we going to go? Are we finally leaving him? I have so many questions that I want to ask her but the words are stuck in my throat.

I take one last look at my room before Mum pulls me down the stairs and along the hallway. We're moving so quickly that I stumble several times and have to grip the bannister to balance myself.

I take large awkward strides along the hallway trying to avoid the shards of broken glass strewn across the floor and this time I don't think this was due to Mum being 'clumsy.'

In the corner near the door, blood is splattered on the wall and carpet. I gasp and my heels dig into the floor. My body refuses to move, but Mum ignores me and just pulls even harder.

I look up as we pass the living room and there he is. Dad stands tall in the doorway. He doesn't look hurt and there's no blood on him so it definitely came from Mum. He always come out of their arguments unharmed. *What have you done?* I ask him with my eyes.

He stares back with a blank expression but his fists are clenched. That's when I notice that one side of his is face is swollen.

Good, I'm glad he's feeling a little pain. It's just a fraction of the pain that he's put Mum through for years and years.

"Come on," Mum says to me.

I look at Dad up and down, I try to speak, but nothing comes out. Why can't I speak? I try again. Nothing.

I can see his chest rising and falling quickly. His breathing is irregular as though he's a toddler trying to calm down. I've never seen him like this before. He usually looks in control of the situation with an amused curl at the side of his lips, as though he is proud of himself, but tonight, he has none of that. He looks almost remorseful. For once, Mum looks like she's the one in control. What has happened?

I step towards Dad. I want to look into his eyes and inspect his swollen face. I want to make sure it really hurts. His eyes brighten and widen as I move closer, but Mum cries, "No!"

She finally pulls me out of the front door.

Where are we going? I want to ask but it's like my voice, along with my peace, has been stolen by the night.

The car is already running, as we step out into the bitterly cold, windy night. We run across the street and Mum slips into the driver's seat.

"Hurry up," she says, already buckling her seatbelt before she's even closed the door.

I jump into the passenger seat and Mum drives off with no hesitation. We're already at the end of the street before I turn around to look back at our house. I can see Dad's silhouette in the front door. He's completely still and watching as we leave.

6

Mum's breathing is fast and erratic. She turns the corner and wipes her eyes with her bandaged hand. She never drives this fast.

I feel nauseous and my stomach is in knots. My face is soaked in tears but at the same time I feel strangely numb.

"Mum, where are we going?" I finally ask in a voice so quiet I hardly recognise myself, but Mum doesn't say anything.

The street lights temporarily shine on her. I can see little hints of her face, like the straightness of her nose, the plump of her lips and the hollows of her eyes. Even in this moment of madness, with mascara down her face and a cut on her cheek and a swollen bloody lip, she's still the most beautiful woman I've ever seen. Her hair is wild and messy and her curls frame her face. She's silently crying but she somehow manages to look stronger than I've ever seen her.

The street lights whizz past and London becomes a blur in the background. Mum reaches out and grabs my hand. I squeeze it and finally, for the first time in months, I feel safe.

AUGUST

ONE

Grandad let me have his room; the best in the house. It's huge, with built-in wardrobes and a bay window with a view of the whole street. I can see right to the park at the end of the road. The street is different to the one we used to live on in London, it's a much busier road and the terrace houses are more tightly packed together.

"She dun need to fall behind inna studies, just because of wh'appen. She gon need a space to work in. It's fine, me 'ardly even in der hennyway," he said to Mum when we first arrived.

I smiled, gratefully. I was shy around him at first. I didn't know him that well and it had taken me a moment to decipher his accent. Despite living in the UK for over sixty years, Grandad still says some words with a thick Jamaican accent and drops some words altogether.

Now, me and Grandad are super close and I wonder how I've even gone through life without seeing him every day. He's so kind and humble. The complete opposite to Dad.

When I was younger we used to come up to Manchester every couple of months to visit Grandad but when Mum would have bald patches in her hair and scratches on her face after fighting with Dad, we stopped. We stopped visiting a lot of people when things started to change at home.

I could see the relief on Mum's face the minute we arrived at Grandad's. It was like the shame and guilt that she had been carrying around instantly melted away.

I love living here. There's no fighting or weird tension. I can breathe.

In the first few months after *that night,* Mum made a few trips back to London with Grandad to collect more stuff from our old house. I hadn't gone with them though; I wasn't ready to see our old life again. But before I knew it, I had missed my chance. There were no more trips back and forth to London anymore. No more chances to confront my dad or see how much he was suffering without us. A few months later, Mum and Dad's divorce was finalised.

When we first got here, I would worry that he was going to turn up and make us go back to London with him. I had nightmares leading up to my sixteenth birthday that he would storm the party, making a scene, but he never came. He didn't even call me to wish me a happy birthday, so I deleted his number. We can both pretend the other doesn't exist.

TWO

I spot my friends Leo and Sanaa as soon as I walk into Fabio's. We've been meeting at the ice cream parlour every Friday since we started at Kemble College and we always manage to get a table by the window.

Leo and Sanaa are sat opposite each other in the booth. Sanaa is waving her hands dramatically and Leo leans back, half listening, half texting as she tells him her latest drama, probably involving some creep who she has been messaging on Instagram.

I walk over, weaving my way through the crowds. I wish I had worn a longer skirt. It's warmer today than I thought it would be and my skirt is sticking to my legs and riding up. It's not really my style, but I've been trying to dress more grown-up in preparation for the final year of college. Apparently, I'm channelling a '*boss bitch*,' as Sanaa so eloquently put it.

When we lived in London, Dad was really strict about what I could wear—nothing short or fitted. It was drilled into me throughout school that I shouldn't wear revealing clothes and I definitely was *not* allowed to spend time with boys. I hate to think what he would do if he saw me hanging out with Leo every day.

I pull at the hem of my skirt and wriggle it down my thighs

before I slide into the booth. Sanaa squeezes my arm in greeting and continues babbling on about something on Instagram.

"I'm going to go and get a banana split," she says when she finally pauses for breath. "What do you guys want?"

"An Oreo milkshake, thanks." Leo orders the same thing all the time.

I pick up the menu to quickly scan it, but I end up just doing what I always do and copying someone else's order.

"Same, thanks."

Leo hands Sanaa a five pound note but she bats his hand away and goes to order.

"What did I miss?" I ask.

He sits up and leans into the table. "Nothing much. Sanaa was just going on about wanting to start a YouTube channel because apparently the Instagram algorithm is messing with her reach." Leo rolls his eyes. "I don't know why she talks to me about this stuff." He starts laughing. His thick eyelashes are giving me a hint of his hazel eyes as the sun catches them. "Like she needs more social media."

Over the summer, Sanaa went completely social media mad. Every second of every day went up on her Instagram stories and she was always on her phone taking pictures or responding to her followers. Her feed is only of her. Either close-ups of her gorgeous face, hot body or the free stuff she gets.

I look over to Sanaa in the queue and, of course, she's on her phone. Probably letting every one of her 200,000-plus followers know that she's in Fabio's having a milkshake.

Leo follows my gaze just as Sanaa holds the phone up to take a selfie. He shakes his head. "I swear I only humour her because she's my cousin."

The bright lights and the red-and-white American style décor in the parlour are so well known all over Manchester that most people do just come here for a decent picture, but Sanaa is obsessed with getting the perfect shot.

"How's everything with you?" I ask as I turn back to Leo. "Were you at football training last night?"

Leo's one of the best players on the college team. He's hoping to get scouted by the time he leaves college so he doesn't have to go to university and become a dentist, like his parents want. He's only got one more year to make a good impression.

"Yeah, it went well. Coach has had a few calls with other teams about me so that's promising." He stares off into the distance.

"Have you said anything to your parents about not wanting to go to uni yet?" I ask, even though I'm sure I already know the answer. I've been encouraging him to talk to his parents all summer.

He shakes his head; making his curls bounce. "No point. Not until I get a contract or at least some real interest from a team."

That familiar look of worry creeps across his face. I've seen this look so many times. He acts like it doesn't kill him to keep his future plans from his parents, but I know it does. His parents are so lovely, I can't even imagine them not being supportive, but Leo says they would freak out if he said he wasn't going down the uni route.

I spot some girls staring over at our table and giggling. I vaguely recognise them from college but I think they're in the year below us. One of them is looking directly at Leo, waiting for him to look up. I discreetly kick him under the table and he looks over to me. I raise my eyebrows and gesture to their table with my eyes. He looks at the chesty brunette waving at him. He waves back coolly, but when he catches my eye, he blushes.

"Check you out with your own fan club!" I tease.

"Whatever. They came to watch us play last night. You know, supporting their college football team, unlike some." He flicks my hand.

"Ow!" I rub the back of my hand. Lately, he's been asking me to come watch him play. Football's not really my scene but I'm running out of excuses. "I'll come soon. It's just I don't like to leave Grandad home alone when Mum's at work."

It's a weak excuse. Grandad is absolutely fine on his own and Leo knows it.

"Mmmm," he says, looking at me sideways.

"I promise." I wag my pinkie finger at him and his links his own to it.

I feel that familiar flutter in my tummy when we touch. He smiles at me. That smile. I blush and pull my finger away.

Did I say that I've had a crush on Leo since the first time Sanaa introduced me to him?

I first met Sanaa in the summer at a College Open Day and we've been inseparable ever since. I remember how she strutted confidently around the hall signing up to classes and chatting to all the teachers as though she had met them before.

I watched in awe, as did everyone else, as she snapped selfies of her herself holding the college prospectus and I laughed when she stood on the stage and pouted into the camera proudly holding her college pass. I remember thinking if she bottles that confidence she'll be a millionaire.

We officially met at the Media Studies stall. She stood next to me and we both asked the tutor questions about the course. Once we were done, she turned to me and said, "Hey I'm Sanaa."

"Amani."

"Cute name. Where you from? Your accent is different."

And that was it. We spent the summer getting to know each other and we loved a lot of the same things. We just clicked and I was so happy I made a friend before college had even started. When she spoke about her *baby* cousin Leo coming back from holiday at the end of summer, I didn't imagine a six-foot, athletic, tanned, fully-grown, drop-dead gorgeous guy!

She must have noticed my delight when I met him for the first time. He slid into the seat opposite us in Fabio's one Saturday afternoon, because she instantly said, "I know what you're thinking and no."

"Why?" I moaned as soon as Leo was out of earshot. Leo was the hottest boy I'd ever seen.

"He's my cousin and you're now my best friend, and if it doesn't work out with you two that would just be messy."

It was the first time Sanaa had referred to me as her best friend. I didn't have any other friends here in Manchester and I wasn't going to throw that away. Even for a hottie like Leo.

"What's taking her so long?" Leo moans.

I look over to the till and spot Sanaa at the front being

served, but she's not focusing on the person behind the till, she's twirling her hair around her finger and talking to Tyler Baxter. I try not to react but my face must have done something because Leo follows my gaze and his jaw instantly tenses. He doesn't like any boys sniffing around Sanaa, especially drug-dealing school-dropouts like Tyler.

"One sec," Leo says before standing up just as Sanaa hands Tyler her phone, clearly exchanging numbers.

Leo walks over to them and grabs the tray with our desserts, dragging Sanaa with him. She has a massive smile on her face and doesn't seem bothered that everyone is staring at her. She loves the attention. I can't help but laugh.

"Did you see that? He just came right over to me," Sanaa says as she slides into the booth. "He said he's messaged me on Insta, but I barely check my DMs anymore, there's so many. I can't believe he likes me!"

She squeezes my hand with excitement. Sanaa always gets attention from boys, way more than I do. Just once I wish I could be the girl meeting a cute guy.

Sanaa coolly looks over to Tyler just as he's leaving Fabio's and holds his gaze. I don't think I've ever seen Tyler Baxter look flustered until now. I watch her in awe. She's such a pro, I honestly don't know how she does it.

"Leo!" Sanaa yells, when she notices that he's drinking his milkshake. "I wanted to take a picture."

"Amani has the exact same drink. Just take a picture of hers."

"Yeah, but three drinks look more aesthetically pleasing." She grabs his milkshake before he can object, putting them in different positions before she takes the picture.

I used to find the whole ordeal annoying, but it's more amusing when Leo's involved.

"Can I drink now?" he snaps.

My phone pings and I already know what it is so I don't bother checking. Of course, it's a notification from Sanaa tagging me on Instagram.

Leo unlocks his phone and reads the caption in a high-pitched, squeaky voice that he thinks resembles Sanaa. "It's Friday so tag your sweet treat binge bestie. . . mine is @ amanibrown." Leo laughs. "You're so cringe man!"

"You're just jealous I didn't tag you." Sanaa sticks her tongue out at him. "Hmmm, what's Tyler's Instagram?"

"Don't you dare," Leo growls and Sanaa laughs.

I smile as I watch them tease each other back and forth before Sanaa's phone pings. I'm so glad I found these two when I moved up here.

"Shit, I've got to go. My nail tech just text saying she has a cancellation." She stands up. "Don't miss me too much darlings!"

She blows us a kiss and rushes to the door leaving Leo and I staring at her banana split. Leo hands me a spare spoon and I don't even question it, we just dive straight in.

THREE

It's almost six by the time we leave Fabio's and it's cooled down outside, which is a welcome change from how humid it's been all day.

"You don't have to walk me home you know," I say to Leo. He checks his phone for the millionth time. "I mean if you have plans, it's cool, it's still early."

A group of girls leave Fabio's giggling and checking out Leo but he doesn't even notice them.

"No, no it's fine. I'm just waiting for a message, but it's cool. Anyways, your grandad would kill me if I let you walk home alone."

He's not wrong, Grandad is always asking Leo to walk me and Sanaa here and there or asking if we're meeting Leo when we go out. He's very old school.

I can feel a smile creeping across my face at the idea of fifteen more minutes alone with Leo. I like spending time with him. I wish I could tell him that but Sanaa has made it clear—many times—that Leo is out of boundaries.

We stop at the end of the road as we wait for the lights to change. I can feel the hairs starting to stand up on the back of my neck as the evening breeze starts to kick in.

"Here." Leo hands me his jacket without even looking at me.

My heart does a little skip and I instantly think of all the movies I've seen where the guy hands the girl his jacket because she feels cold and this marks the point where he lets her know he's interested in being more than friends. Except Leo says nothing and he has never told me that he likes me as more than a friend. So, I'm clearly just letting my imagination run away with me *again*.

He looks at me and up and down. "The jacket suits you."

I wish I had something charming or witty to say but instead I just blush.

The high-rise apartments being built next to my street seem to be growing a couple of feet taller every day. Grandad thinks they're going up too quickly and a gust of wind will bring them down. He said we're living in a 'hollow country' and I can't help but think he's referring to the people rather than the buildings.

We walk by the construction site in silence. Although it's cooled down now and my thighs can breathe, my skirt is still twisting around. I keep stopping every few seconds to fiddle with it and pull it down. I try to do it quickly so that Leo doesn't notice.

A couple walk towards us and we're forced to squeeze up on the narrow pavement to let them pass. My body brushes Leo as we tuck to the side next to a fence. We're so close I can feel the heat from Leo's body and my body tingles.

I adjust my skirt for the millionth time, but this time he notices. He very obviously looks down at my thighs before he catches himself and looks away. This time he's the one to blush.

He coughs clearing his throat. "You going to Kerry's party tomorrow night?"

"I wasn't planning to. I have some reading to do for English Lit."

Leo laughs. "Amani, college isn't for another few weeks!"

"I know but I like to be prepared," I say defensively. "But Sanaa has been begging me to go all week. You know what she's like, she can't miss an event."

"Facts."

"You?"

Leo pauses. He's not a huge fan of parties and he hates drinking. The hangover makes him miss a day of training.

"I might just have to make an appearance, to look after you two—as usual." He playfully nudges me.

He's referring to that one time when Sanaa and I drank too much at a house party and Sanaa ended up arguing with some random girls over something stupid. Leo dragged us away from them and we threw up on the pavement and he was left to sort us out. Real classy.

We're a few doors from my house and I don't want the walk to be over. I turn to Leo and he's already looking at me, well, my legs.

"New?" he nods towards my skirt.

"Yeah, I mean no—Sanaa gave it to me."

"I was thinking I've never seen you wear that before. It looks good on you though."

What does he mean by good? Does he mean good compared to how I usually look? Does he mean I actually look good? Do I usually look bad?

He must hear me thinking because he says, "I mean, not like you don't always look good. It's just usually you wear baggier clothes."

"So, you prefer me in short, tight clothes?" I bravely tease.

He laughs nervously and shakes his head. "I just meant. . . you always look good to me, Amani."

Before I even have a chance to respond, Grandad opens the front door.

"Leo, good to see yuh, son."

"Good to see you too," he responds. "Amani's going to bring you to my next football match."

"Maybe," I slip in quickly.

"We'll be dere. Let us kno' when. Maybe yuh mum would even come?"

Grandad's always trying to get Mum to do things with us, but we both know she won't. She's either working or she says she's tired. Grandad says she works too hard but I think it's more than that. She's in bed for days sometimes, not even eating a meal with us, and I don't think that's normal.

"Maybe," I respond. "Thanks for walking me home. I'll see you at Kerry's tomorrow."

His phone pings and he grabs it out of his pocket and just like that I've lost his attention.

"Yeah, tomorrow, bye," he says backing off and texting.

I follow Grandad into the house and smile to myself remembering Leo fumbling around his words. *"You always look good to me, Amani."* I replay the words over and over in my head. All I want to do is call Sanaa and ask her what she thinks he means. She's better at this kind of thing. But it's Leo, so I can't.

As Grandad wanders off into the kitchen, I lean my head back against the front door. If Dad was here he would have lost it if Leo walked me home, like that time with Callum.

FOUR

Life with Dad

"Who was that?" Dad has one hand on his hip and one on the doorframe blocking me from passing him.

"A friend," I answer quickly.

His nostrils are flared and his jaw is tight, but I'm not sure why. I know he doesn't want me having a boyfriend while I'm at school, but surely, he can't be against me having boys who are just friends?

I watch his face closely; the tightness of his jaw makes me nervous.

"Who was that?" he repeats each word more slowly.

"Callum, he lives up the street." I know he wants more information but I don't want to give him anything else. I don't want him to figure out that Callum is potentially going to be my boyfriend soon, if things go to plan.

I push past him and make my way up to my bedroom, keeping one eye on him as I mount the stairs two at a time. I can see his chest rising and falling as he watches me. My palms instantly begin to sweat. Where's Mum?

The minute I get to the top of the stairs, I race across the hallway out of sight. I close my bedroom door quickly and let out a sigh of relief. I press my ear to the door but I can't hear Dad's footsteps following me. Thank God.

I go to my window and watch Callum walk down the street. The trees which line the pavement block him at points so I twist my neck to try and watch him for as long as possible. I wonder what he's thinking? I wonder if he wanted to kiss me? Oh, I hope so.

Maybe the last few Fridays that my friend, Tash, has spent laying my baby hairs while I rolled up my school skirt before walking home with Callum have paid off. Maybe I'm finally going to get a boyfriend.

I want to tell Tash that Callum walked me home, but before I can even scroll through my phone to find her name, Dad bursts through the door, reaches me in two long strides and grabs my wrist.

"Ouch, you're hurting me!" I wail, trying to twist my wrist out of his grasp.

"What have I told you about running the streets with boys?" His grip on my wrist tightens. I look him dead in the eyes. He hates me right now, I can tell. "Have some self-respect. Do you know what people will say about girls like you? Don't bring boys to my door, Amani!"

I wince with the pain but he doesn't loosen up. A vein is pulsing out of his head and he has tiny beads of sweat forming around his hairline. He looks like he's going to explode.

"Do you understand me?" He twists my wrist and it burns. I lean in to the pain.

Don't cry! Don't give him the satisfaction. I keep my eyes steady and stare into his dead eyes.

"Yes Dad."

He finally lets go of my wrist and walks out, slamming my bedroom door behind him so hard that the room shakes. I collapse into a heap on the floor, cradling my sore wrist and let the tears finally fall. I never let Callum walk me home again.

FIVE

Sanaa waits on the corner outside Boots for me, just as we planned. Her long loose curls swing around her shoulders as she holds her phone up at an angle and tries to find the right lighting for the perfect selfie. She doesn't even notice the group of boys stumbling over each other as they walk by to try to get a good look at her. I roll my eyes. She's wearing her *'booty'* jeans and I realise in that moment exactly how they got their name.

I walk towards her, feeling slightly less *'booty'* in my jeans that don't hug me in the same way. I tug on my baggy t-shirt and pull it below my bum. She doesn't see me approaching because she's so distracted in trying to look cute while pouting. I admire the effort.

"Those jeans? Really?" I ask as I get closer.

She turns and giggles, sliding her phone into her pocket. She throws her arms around me and my face gets lost in a cloud of curls. She smells so good, fruity and expensive—she must have used her mum's hair products again. I smile, remembering the drama she caused last time when she wasted all of her mum's products.

"I just thought I would make the effort for a day of shopping with my best girl!" She pulls away from me and looks at me up and down. "Can I try something?"

She doesn't wait for me to respond. She grabs the hem at the back of my t-shirt and ties it up into a knot so that my top sits just above my waist. I'm flashing a bit of my stomach, but not too much. I look down, impressed with the transformation.

"And now you look very sexy. I don't understand why you don't show all of this!" She smacks my bum making me jump. "Your figure is fire! Guys would die to get their hands on it."

I smile to myself remembering Leo telling me how good I looked in my skirt. Maybe she has a point?

We walk inside Boots and Sanaa leads us straight to the makeup aisle. I instantly feel lost. Dad never let me wear makeup so I've only just about mastered concealer and mascara; the rest is still a mystery.

Sanaa swipes a scarlet red lipstick on the back of her hand, which looks stunning against her golden complexion. She holds her hand up to the light.

"I think it's too bright." She puts the tester back, grabs a darker shade and repeats the process.

I refrain from sighing—they will all look good against her skin; they were made to. She grabs my hand and tests it on the back of my hand.

"Now that looks sick." She holds my hand up closer to my face and I'm surprised. It does look good. "You have to get it. In fact, I'll get it for you." She puts her hands in prayer position. "Please, let me get it for you. It'll look so good on you when I do your make up later."

"Okay fine, but I don't want anything OTT. I wanna—"

"Still look like you, yeah, yeah I know." Sanaa rolls her eyes. She grabs a couple of strip lashes and continues browsing the shelves. "So, I have something to tell you."

We join the back of the queue.

"What's up?"

"I met up with Tyler after I left Fabio's!" She squeals and clasps her hands over her mouth, like his name accidentally slipped out.

"Tyler Baxter!" I shout and all four of the customers in front of us turn and look. I know exactly what they're thinking, '*loud, obnoxious, Black teens,*' but for once I don't care.

"Tell me everything!" I grip her by both shoulders "Did you. . . you know?"

"What?" Sanaa steps away from me. "Amani! What kind of girl do you think I am?"

"Oh sorry, I didn't mean it like that." Sanaa's the last person I want to offend.

She laughs. "Who am I kidding? I wouldn't have said no if he offered."

We both break into a fit of giggles.

"So, what happened? I'm guessing Leo doesn't know yet?"

"No, Leo is definitely not finding out so keep it shut, Marns!" She points at me. "He will just fly off the handle and ruin it. Leo's judged Tyler based on stupid rumours and it's not fair."

"Oh, so it was all rumours? He doesn't sell weed and he wasn't kicked out of college?"

"Oh no, he most definitely sells weed and he was kicked out of Kemble for it, but come on, who doesn't sell weed nowadays?"

Me and you I want to say, but I don't.

"The only difference is Tyler got caught." She shrugs as though it's no big deal. "Anyway, I gave him my number in

Fabio's, he texted me and asked me to meet him. He said he wanted to talk. So, when I left, I met him in his car, and he was like, come for a ride with me."

"Wait, so he can drive legally?" She nods. "How old is he?" I sound like my dad.

"Seventeen, but you're allowed to drive with a provisional license. He drove me to The Edge."

"The Edge?" I know that's a place where people go to have sex.

"You know that posh part of Stockport? You can walk up and literally look out across the whole of Manchester."

I feel like she's making it sound better than it is.

"So, the sex spot?"

Sanaa swats my arm. "Marns, shut up! It was so romantic. We watched as the sun set and he gave me his jacket, which kind of confirmed that he was legit into me. I mean he was dropping compliments all night. It was so sweet. He just draped it over my shoulder. He didn't even ask, he just knew what I needed." She stares into the distance and I'm sure I've lost her in Tyler Land. "We kissed and talked and he dropped me home. Then, when he got home, he called and we spoke on the phone all night. I've had like three hours sleep, if that."

She's glowing as she talks about Tyler and her already animated mannerisms become even more exaggerated. I love seeing her so happy, but I can't help but think that this is exactly how she behaves every time a guy gives her attention, even if he doesn't treat her right. I hope Tyler is going to treat her better.

As we're finally being served, I can't help but think about

Leo draping his jacket over my shoulders. Maybe it did mean something more?

"I can't wear this."

Despite spending two hours in town looking for something to wear, I'm still stressing about what to wear to the party tonight. I don't even want to go now.

Sanaa pulls another mini dress out of her wardrobe. "What about this?" she asks.

The dress is black and has tiny pink zigzags all over it. I stare at it for a minute and wonder what I can team it with. I don't know why I'm bothering because Sanaa is already going through her excessive jewellery collection. She hands me the dress and some gold hoops. The dress still has the tags on, so it must have been gifted.

"Aren't you a bit overdressed?"

Sanaa looks at her tight, silver, slinky dress with spaghetti straps as if seeing it for the first time.

"Hmm, maybe but I'm late on posting this dress."

A minute later I'm in the zigzag dress and it actually looks really good. I force my feet into my black sandals just as Sanaa walks over and dangles some gold chains around my neck.

Sanaa puts on a pair of high-top, platform Converse and somehow it works. I could never.

"Come sit down." Sanaa takes the glue and applies them to the lash strip and holds them in place. She applies a light blush and eyeshadow and finally the lipstick that she got for me. She stands back and looks at me before she smiles. "I'm so damn good at this."

I look in the mirror and I'm taken aback. I can never understand how she manages to make my face look like this.

Sanaa hands me a shot glass of rum. "Cheers."

We clink glasses and I swallow it down, pulling a face as it burns my throat.

"Let me just do my hair and we can go."

I look at the clock on her wall and it's already 10:25pm. Thankfully, it's the summer holidays and as long as I'm home by midnight, I'll be fine. I sit on the bed and pull my phone out of my backpack. I've still got Leo's jacket in there; I smell it as I reach in and there's something so comforting about it. I text him to let him know we'll be there soon.

Sanaa joins me on the bed and I quickly push the jacket back further into my bag.

"How's your mum doing? I've not seen her in a while."

"Oh," I say taken aback. "Yeah, she's taken on some extra shifts at the hospital so she's not around much."

Sanaa came to my house last weekend and I told her Mum was at work. The truth is she was in bed where she had been all weekend.

I stand up from the bed wanting to move on from the conversation. Sanaa gets the hint and jumps up.

"Let's take a selfie." She pulls me in so that our cheeks almost touch and holds the phone up at an angle and clicks furiously, trying to capture the perfect image. "Got it." She shows me and Sanaa is all shiny and gorgeous and I'm smiling but I can see the sadness in my eyes.

We take another shot before one last glance in the mirror and we're out the door.

SIX

The party is rammed. Everyone is drinking from plastic cups and shouting to be heard above the music. The bass is pumping hard and it's making the adrenaline rush through my veins. The rum is helping me feel less tense.

Sanaa weaves through the crowd, greeting everybody, and I follow behind smiling at a few people that I recognise. The plastic bag holding our rum and vodka for the night hits my ankles with each step and I can feel the bottles clanging together.

We find the kitchen and grab a couple of plastic cups. A pretty tipsy, ginger-haired guy presses up to Sanaa and smiles. "Sanaa, right? You're looking good."

She turns her back on the guy, dismissing him, and proceeds to pour the drinks. He gives her a dirty look before walking off.

We down a cup of rum and Coke and immediately pour another. I look around the sea of vaguely familiar faces from college. No sign of Leo.

"Let's go into the living room and see who's here," Sanaa says, grabbing my hand.

I try not to spill my drink as we walk through the crowds and she taps someone whose face I can't see.

"Hey, have you seen Tyler?" she shouts to be heard above the blaring music.

Great, she's waiting for Tyler, so now I'm going to be the third wheel. I hate when she does this.

"Tyler's coming?" I shout above the music. It comes out more hostile than I wanted it to.

"Yeah, it's cool, he's cool, you'll like him."

But I don't feel reassured. I'm pissed. I would have stayed home, done my reading and caught up on a Netflix series if I knew I was chaperoning. I cross my arms across my chest.

The guy she tapped is watching us with a smile on and I catch my breath when I clock who it is. It's Ryan Bailey!

I get an instant flashback of how he walked into Sociology last year, in my first week at Kemble, with a fresh pair of Jordan's and a twinkle in his eye. He asked if I had a spare pen and I couldn't concentrate on anything we were learning in class after that.

He bends down and whispers something into Sanaa's ear and jealousy jolts through my body seeing him that close to her. She smiles and whispers back and he responds with a shrug. He looks away from Sanaa and his eye drifts over to me. I smile and instantly start to fiddle with my hair. He nods at me before turning back around.

That is the most interaction I've had with Ryan since I lent him a pen last year. I sigh at how pathetic I am.

Sanaa texts quickly, I'm sure it's to Tyler. She drains her cup. "Come on, keep up."

I've had enough. I don't see the point in drinking anymore when I'm going to be on my own in less than an hour. As soon as Tyler gets here Sanaa will leave me alone while they sneak off claiming they will "be back in a sec."

"Hey girls," a deep, familiar voice says.

Sanaa's eyes widen. "I thought you weren't coming?"

"What, and leave you two here alone getting drunk? Besides Amani practically begged me to come," Leo says.

I blush and shake my head. Sanaa glares at me.

"Where are the drinks? I wanna get a Coke." He smiles, oblivious to Sanaa's discomfort.

I point towards the kitchen.

"Damn girl, why didn't you tell me?" Sanaa rounds on me as soon as Leo's gone. "I invited Tyler and Leo's going to ruin it. He threatened to tell my mum I'm seeing a drug dealer if he sees me with him again."

"Can't you just tell Tyler not to come?"

"He's already on his way, he'll be here in five." She sighs. "I just wanna spend some time with him and figure out if there's a real spark between us." Her eyes light up. "What we need is more shots! I'm gonna need them."

We rush back through the crowd to the kitchen where she pours us a double, mixing the rum and the vodka that we took from her mum's house. I know mixing the two isn't smart and I regret it when I drink it down. I chase it up with Coke.

Sanaa's phone pings and she gasps. "He's here." She fluffs up her hair and her curls effortlessly fall into place. "I want you to meet him"

I don't want to meet him. Not that I don't like Tyler but Sanaa never stays in a relationship for long. She has no idea how exhausting it is getting to know them and then having to shut them out once they break up. I wish we could just enjoy the party—just me, her and Leo—before the summer ends. But it's like the alcohol has slowed down my speech and before I can object, Sanaa is pulling me out to the front of the house.

We stand in the front garden for a few moments, watching girls stumbling over the grass and groups of people recording themselves drinking and singing along to the music. It's a warm August night, perfect for the last party of the summer.

There are empty plastic cups and balloon canisters strewn across the grass and path. I can't help but think that it's only a matter of time before one of the neighbours calls the police and I don't want to be around when that happens. I swallow hard trying to work out how drunk I am. I want to be sober enough to make a swift exit if I need to.

"Hey beautiful." Tyler makes his way up the path to Sanaa. A couple of the girls in the garden stop and stare. I completely understand why.

Sanaa has to tip-toe to reach her arms around his neck and hug him. He's dressed in a tight black t-shirt that shows off his muscles and he appears to be much older than seventeen. He stands out from the other boys at the party, not only because he's twice their size but his trainers and gold chain look expensive.

"This is my friend, Amani." She points to me.

"Hey." He smiles, flashing a gold tooth. Up close he's not actually as attractive as I thought, but Sanaa doesn't seem to notice. She's not stopped smiling since he called her *beautiful*.

He holds her at arm's length and looks her up and down biting his lip. He looks so into her. I try not to show how jealous I am by pretending not to see him pulling her in for a hug. Truth is though, that's what I want—a guy who wraps his arms around me in public and holds me while smothering me in compliments. I want to know what it feels like to grin from ear to ear and stare into someone's eyes, knowing that they want nothing more than to kiss me.

Tyler bends down and lines Sanaa's jaw with little kisses and she laughs. I look away and pull my phone out so I don't look like that awkward friend. I want to go back inside, but I stay to show Sanaa that I'm happy for her. Not that she even notices me.

I scroll through Instagram trying to look busy. I hear the music inside switch to Jorja Smith and I start swaying side to side. I feel stupid.

"Dancing alone?" a voice comes from behind me.

I look up from my phone and turn around. It's Ryan Bailey. I take a deep breath and push my phone into my pocket. I turn back to check on Sanaa but she's already moved further towards the other side of the garden. Thanks for letting me know.

"Where's your mate? Leo's cousin—what's she called?"

I should have known that he was only talking to me to find out where Sanaa is. I point to her and Tyler.

He looks over and nods, but surprisingly he doesn't actually seem that bothered about Sanaa.

I feel my hands clam up and I'm holding my stomach in and arching my back. I've seen Sanaa do it in photos. Ryan lights a cigarette and holds it out to me. I shake my head and he shrugs. He leans against the wall with one foot up and blows out a puff of smoke. I try not to cough as I inhale some of it.

"Amani, right?" I nod. How does he know my name? "You don't talk much, do you?"

I try to respond but nothing comes out. Almost as though I'm trying to prove his point. I shrug and smile.

The street light illuminates his face. His hair is shaved short and his blue eyes sparkle through the puffs of smoke.

"So, what's the deal with her and Tyler then?" Ryan looks over to Sanaa.

Maybe I was wrong, he is bothered about Sanaa.

"They're just getting to know each other," I respond, just as Sanaa pulls Tyler in for a proper kiss.

Ryan laughs and a small puff of smoke escapes from between his lips. "It seems like they know each other pretty well. Does Leo know?" He laughs again and I can't help but join him because I know what he's getting at.

I shake my head. It's a bit weird that he's asking about Leo since they don't really seem to get along. They're on the same football team, but from what Leo has said they're only mates on the pitch because they have to be. Maybe he just likes the idea of Leo getting wound up about Tyler.

"Fuck, I wouldn't want my little cousin running around with him. I mean he's a nice enough guy, but I wouldn't want him messing around with my family, you know?"

He looks at me and I nod. I suddenly feel like I should warn Sanaa, not like she'll listen. He presses his cigarette against the wall just as Leo walks out of the house. Shit!

Ryan and I look at each other, and I can see the amusement in his face.

"Leo, over here!" he shouts across the garden.

Leo makes his way over. I can see that he doesn't really want to, but then he spots me and I'm sure I see his eyes brighten. As he approaches us, his back is thankfully to Sanaa. The last thing I want is for him and Sanaa to get into a massive argument. I hate when people shout at each other.

"Hey, you alright?" he looks from me to Ryan and frowns. "Where's Sanaa?"

"Toilet," I say quickly at the same time Ryan says, "Getting a drink."

I don't know why Ryan responded but he smirks. Leo looks him up and down. I look to where Sanaa was but she seems to have slipped out of the gate with Tyler. Great, now where did she go? I don't know Tyler well and the idea of him and Sanaa alone in the night makes me feel uneasy.

"She went to get a drink and then use the toilet," I explain. "Oh, here's your jacket."

I take it from my bag hand it to him.

"Thanks. And you stayed talking with him? I didn't even know you two knew each other." He points towards Ryan.

"We're getting to know each other." Ryan winks at me and Leo's not the only one who's confused. He's spoken more about Sanaa than me.

"Let's go and find Sanaa," I say. "Nice chatting to you Ryan."

Ryan nods at me. Leo's swaying a little and stumbles over his feet, which is strange as he doesn't drink.

Where is Sanaa? I could kill her for this. I lead Leo upstairs and we sit at the top of the stairs where there are less people. I shoot a quick text to Sanaa asking where she is. Thankfully, she responds straight away.

SANAA: *Don't worry, I'll be back in 10 x*

"Ryan?" Leo says.

"Huh?" I put my phone away.

Only then do I notice the bottle in his hand. Is he drinking? I've never seen Leo drink before.

He follows my gaze and flashes me an apologetic smile. "It's been a long day. So what's with you and Ryan?"

"He was just keeping me company while I waited for Sanaa. You're not jealous, are you?" I playfully nudge him.

Leo laughs and takes another swig from his bottle. "Do you want me to be?" He raises his eyebrows. Before I can even answer, he adds, "It's good to see you being more chill. It's just. . . Ryan Bailey." He snorts.

"What's wrong with him?"

"What's right with him? He's only after one thing and I don't think you're up for it."

"Is that right?" I glare at him. Is he implying I'm frigid?

"You're closed up," Leo says, clearly not seeing how pissed I am. "Is it because of the way your dad was with you? Sanaa told me he was really protective so you've never really dated."

Images of my dad quickly flash across my mind. Dad raising his fists and Mum cowering away from him. Dad grabbing my wrists and twisting them. I look down at my wrist and I feel like it's burning.

"You don't know anything," I hiss and Leo recoils.

"Amani, I didn't mean to be rude. You've taken it the wrong way."

The house is literally shaking with the base and the crowd are all swaying in sync to the music. Everything feels too loud. I need to get out of here.

"I'm gonna grab a drink." But instead of going into the kitchen, I'm out of the front door and I don't stop walking until I get to the end of the street and the music is a distant thump.

The tears follow and they don't stop. I try to take a deep

breath but it hurts. I grip my chest and pull at the dress. I feel like I'm suffocating. Why did he need to bring up Dad?

I close my mouth and try breathing just through my nose but it's no use. I grip my chest again and sit on the edge of the pavement. I close my eyes and my breathing slows down and starts to return to normal.

I pull off my fake lashes and throw them on the pavement. After a moment, I stand up and start walking home, trying not to think about anything and especially not Dad.

SEVEN

Life with Dad

I wake up and instantly put my hands over my ears. I don't want to hear it anymore. I'm sick of the screaming and arguing. There's an undeniable slapping sound and for a second the screaming stops.

Mum starts wailing. Dad shouts over her screams. I plug my ears with my fingers.

"I'VE HAD ENOUGH!" I scream into the darkness.

I instantly clasp my hands over my mouth. My muscles tense up. I can't believe I just did that.

There's silence throughout the entire house. I wait. Then, heavy, familiar footsteps storm out of my parent's room.

I squeeze my eyes shut and prepare myself for Dad to burst through the door. I pull the quilt up over my face. But the footsteps don't get any closer, instead he heads down the stairs and into his office. The office door slams shut.

I lie still in case he changes his mind. After a while, I finally exhale, feeling lightheaded from holding my breath.

SEPTEMBER

EIGHT

I'm up early the next day. My throat is dry and my head is killing me. I couldn't sleep all night thinking about what Leo said. Am I closed up? Is that what everyone thinks about me?

I pull off my pyjamas and throw on a sports bra and tracksuit. I have an urge to get outside. I pop my earphones in and as the relaxing sound of Brent Faiyaz gently floods through my ears. I feel the tension in my shoulders drift away. If there's anything that's going to shift this hangover and clear my head it's music and a quick run around the park. I used to run loads in London. Any excuse to get out of the house.

The house is quiet. I walk down the corridor and gently open Mum's bedroom door. Mum's curled up in the corner of the bed gently breathing. The room smells musty, like damp clothes. I want to open the window but I'm scared of waking her up. Instead, I grab the empty mugs that are on the floor and pull the door closed.

I dump the cups in the kitchen sink, grab a bottle of water and head out. The air is crisp and fresh. Perfect weather for a run. I set off jogging towards the park, which is deserted, just the way I like it. I pick up the pace as Beyoncé bleeds into my ears and I'm grateful that it drowns out any thoughts of last night. I'm breathing heavy now and my chest is opening up. I feel good.

Once I've done a few laps, I head towards the exit. A tall, dark-skinned man passes me as I cross the road back toward the house. He briefly looks at me and quickly looks away. I whip my head around to get a better look. Dad? I stand still, watching him walk away, willing him to turn around just so I can be sure, but he doesn't. All I can do is watch until he disappears into the distance.

"You need to be more careful Amani. You nearly burnt the whole house down!"

After sleeping in pretty late Mum's woken up in a bad mood. She throws the burnt scrambled eggs I made us in the bin. She balances on a chair wafting smoke out of the tiny open window in the kitchen.

"I can do that." I reach out to help her down of the chair. Smoke continues filling the kitchen, moving violently in all directions. She ignores my hand and I drop it, feeling incapable.

"Shut that door!" She gestures towards the kitchen door.

"I know, but I was just—"

"Yeah, you said you were just trying to make some eggs, but you should have been paying attention."

Mum steps down from the chair and blasts the frying pan with cold water in the sink.

"I got side-tracked and you were tired." I argue. "I was making them for you." I want to see her actually eating something but I can't tell her that.

"Marni." Mum pauses and turns to face me. She looks

exhausted, this is a permanent look lately. "Just pay attention, okay? I start my shift at the hospital soon so I'll grab food there."

I roll my eyes knowing that "I'll grab food there" is code for a cup of coffee.

"Mum you're working too hard. How about I find a part time job to help out?"

Mum shakes her head. "If you want to help out, you just need to focus on college and getting into uni."

I swallow hard. "I'm worried about you."

Mum freezes and just for a second I think she's going to open up to me but then she plasters on a forced smile. "I'm fine. Now can I tidy up in peace please?"

Reluctantly, I walk into the living room and flop down on the sofa. Why won't she talk to me? I feel like we only ever talk about school or chores, like I can't get through to her about anything deeper than that. It's frustrating feeling like I'm constantly walking on eggshells.

My phone buzzes with back to back messages from Leo asking me what happened last night.

"You happened last night," I say to my phone.

"How were the eggs?" Grandad asks as he walks into the living room.

I can still smell the smoke, so I know he already knows the answer. "Burnt."

He laughs. "Where's your mum?"

"Getting ready for work." I shrug not wanting to talk anymore.

Grandad sighs and it speaks volumes. Mum doesn't open up to him either.

My phone vibrates again but this times it's Sanaa calling. I ignore it. I'm not in the mood to hear about Tyler. All I want to know is why she's talking about Dad to Leo when I told her that stuff in private.

"How's your mum been this week?" Grandad asks, breaking my train of thought.

"The same, pretty much."

Grandad's shoulders droop and he stares off into the distance. I know we both have the same constant worry. Like me, he wants to know what he can do to make everything better and I wish I had the answer.

NINE

"Amani, wait up!" Sanaa runs to catch up with me. "What happened to you? You've not replied to a single one of my messages."

"Sorry, busy weekend," I lie.

I knew she would pretend that she hadn't ditched me at the party.

"Oh, okay, everything cool at home?" She links her arm through mine and looks at me as we walk towards college.

I don't know what I prefer—busy Sanaa who doesn't even look at me when she's speaking and insists on documenting everything we do on social media, or this Sanaa, who is super intense and wants details about everything. I know she means well, but I'm not in the mood to go into specifics about Mum, especially on the first day back to college.

"Good," I lie again.

Luckily, that's all it takes for her to completely drop it and move on.

"Look at this." She shoves her phone in my face. "The comments are crazy in the pic with me and Tyler."

I scroll through and see 'loser,' 'wasteman,' 'drug-dealer.'

"I spent all weekend deleting comments but they just keep coming. You like Tyler, right?"

"Well, I don't really know him." I say carefully. "Has he seen this?"

Sanaa nods. "He thinks I overshare."

I can't help but laugh. "He does know you right?"

"Maybe I should tone it down?"

"You shouldn't change who you are for a guy."

Sanaa bites her lip and I shake my head. Sanaa is always changing herself for boys.

We head into the building and after I promise to catch her at lunch, I head to Double English.

"Glad to see you're still alive," Leo says as I slide into the table in front of him.

"Alive and kicking," I say dryly.

"Listen, I'm sorry about what I said at the party. I was drunk and not thinking. I didn't mean to upset you."

Our teacher, Mr Becker, enters the room and starts fumbling with his bag.

"We'll talk at lunch time yeah?" I say and Leo nods.

My phone vibrates in my pocket and I reach under the table to have a look at it.

MUM: *Come straight home after college, please. We need to talk xx*

What is that about? My mind immediately goes to Grandad. Is he okay? I feel my heart rate double. Why has she sent such a cryptic message?

I spend the rest of the lesson nervously fumbling with the ends of my braids and wondering what could be so important that Mum needs me home straight after college. I barely hear anything that Mr Becker is saying. I'm so relieved when the bell goes for lunch and I immediately dart out of the classroom.

I run straight outside and sit on the steps. I try to call Mum but there's no answer. I swallow hard.

Don't panic, she'll call back.

I wait, checking my phone. I text her but there's no response.

Should I go home now? I shake my head. I'm overreacting. If it was that important, she would have told me to come home straight away. Before I know it the bell rings and it's time for Sociology. I pick up my bag and head back inside, hoping not to bump into Leo or Sanaa on my way to class. I don't want to have to lie again about why I missed having lunch with them.

After college I spot Sanaa by the steps.

"Hey, you ready to go? I've got to rush home."

Sanaa places her hands on her hips and she's looking at me up and down.

I feel butterflies rising in my tummy. Why is she staring at me like that?

"Amani, what is going on with you? First, you completely ignore me and Leo all weekend and sorry but no-one is that busy to respond to one text. Then you tell us you'll come and talk to us at lunchtime and don't even show up."

A lump forms in my throat and I automatically begin to fiddle with the end of one of my braids. I don't really have a response.

"I just. . . it's just. . ."

"Yeah, we know, you have a lot going on, but who doesn't? I'm trying to figure things out with Tyler, and Leo is stressed about uni, but we're functioning and communicating. Leo said you ditched him at the party on Saturday, what's all that about?"

She doesn't even pause for an answer, but if she had, I would have told her that she wasn't really in a position to talk about ditching friends at parties and maybe she shouldn't be sharing my secrets with people.

"I mean we're your friends! You're supposed to tell us things and talk to us. Honestly, since your mum started getting depressed you hardly talk to us. You're going to end up just like her if you're not careful. That's how it begins. All that bottling things up isn't good."

Anyone else would have slapped her for saying that, but I've been around enough of that to last me a lifetime. And I refuse to be like my dad.

I look around to see if anyone's looking. She isn't shouting but she's making a bit of a scene and waving her arms about. I can feel my body getting sweaty. I can't deal with this right now. I just need to get home to Mum. I take a deep breath.

"My mum's not depressed," it comes out in a hissed whisper. "And I'm not depressed either."

"I didn't say you are, but you *will* be if you don't open up and stop leaving your friends in the dark. We only want to help."

Help? Is she joking? Does she think this is helping?

I swallow hard as my throat feels dry. A group of girls from our year walk by giggling and chatting loudly. They smile at us but I'm not in the mood to even attempt to smile back. My eyes are welling up. There's absolutely no way I'm about to cry right now. I do *not* cry in public.

"I try to talk to you Sanaa, all the time. You're so wrapped up in being Insta-famous and now sneaking around with your drug-dealer boyfriend that you don't even listen. You've always got one eye on your phone and one earphone in! What's the point in talking to someone if they don't care?" As soon as I stop talking I regret every word. I shake my head, wishing I can take it all back. "Sanaa, I didn't mean that."

I reach out to touch her hand and she pulls away.

"Do you know what Marns, you're right. I'm an awful friend. I'm selfish and self-indulgent and I clearly don't care about you at all. Thank you for letting me know. Have fun finding a better friend who wants to be constantly pushed away and reminded that they're not good enough! Let me know when you find that friend who makes all the effort and gets nothing in return."

She walks away from me and I want her to come back but the words won't form. I'm stuck to the step, unable to move, just like I was *that night* when I stood at the top of the stairs.

I feel like I can't take a deep breath. The air keeps getting trapped in my chest. What's happening to me?

I. Can't. Breathe.

I grip my chest and try to calm myself down. I clasp my hands together and count to ten.

1. . . 2. . . 3. . . 4. . . 5. . . 6.

It's getting worse.

7. . . 8 . . . 9. . . 10.

I sit on the step and close my eyes.

Just breathe, just breathe, just breathe. Come on Amani.

1. . . 2. . . 3. . . 4. . . 5. . . 6. . . 7.

"Hey, you alright? Do you want me to get someone?" I don't open my eyes but I can hear that the voice is coming from above me.

I prise one eye open and look at the ground. I can see their shoes. Fresh, white Jordan's. I already know it's Ryan Bailey.

"Hey, can you hear me?" he asks gently.

I look up him and I'm surprised that he's searching my face for answers. He looks worried, concerned even. I attempt to stand up and steady myself with one hand on the wall but I wobble and Ryan grabs my arm to steady me.

"Do you want me to find someone? Are you waiting for Sanaa?"

People are bounding up and down the stairs. I somehow tuned them all out until now.

Deep breath, Amani.

"Yes, no," I splutter realising I hadn't answered his question.

"Well, which one?" he smiles. He has a dimple on his left cheek. Oh God, he's beautiful.

"Sorry, yes, I'm fine and no I'm not waiting for Sanaa. She's already left. I need to get home."

"Oh right, well, let me walk with you."

He swings my heavy bag over his shoulder and holds out his arm. For a moment I'm confused and then I realise that he wants me to link arms with him. What is happening?

I link my arm through his and we walk down the college steps together. A group of girls from our year look over and start whispering among themselves. Great. They must have seen me sitting with my eyes closed on the steps, God knows what they think of me now. I glance over at them and they're not looking at me, they're looking at Ryan, who's carrying my bag.

I reach up to grab it from him, feeling embarrassed.

"Feeling better?" he asks as I take the bag from him.

"Yeah, thanks—you don't have to carry my bag for me," I say blushing.

"I wanted to." He looks directly at me and I swear I melt a little. "So, you wanna tell me what happened?"

We walk through the college gates on to the street. Neither of us stop walking as we pass a group of guys kicking an empty plastic bottle.

"Ryan," calls out one boy in a blue hoodie, as if inviting him to join.

Ryan shakes his head and gestures to me. They all look at me and smile, one waves so I wave back. I don't recognise any of them. Did Ryan Bailey just turn down his friends to walk with me?

"So, what happened?" Ryan asks again.

"I just couldn't breathe properly."

"My sister used to have panic attacks all the time when she was younger. She used to do this thing where she tried to find five objects to focus on that were the same colour." He looks around. "That leaf, his bag." He points to the guy in front of us with the green backpack. "The grass, that bike." He looks frantically around for something else green before he looks at himself and laughs. "My jacket."

I'm surprised that he can relate to what I'm going through. Ryan seems to walk around without a care in the world.

"The idea is it takes your mind off your breathing, so you focus on something else and then your breathing can get back to normal. You should try it next time."

He waves at a girl standing by a car. She waves back and then looks at me up and down. She's blonde and has legs for days in her mini-skirt. She tilts her head to the right and scrunches up her nose showing her blatant confusion about Ryan walking with me. To be honest, I'm confused about why he's walking with me too.

He lights up a cigarette and just like the other night he offers me one. I shake my head.

"I'm trying to quit. Coach said I could improve my stamina if I kick it. I'm down to three a day. Sorry, I'm just waffling on, it's just you don't talk much, do you?"

I nod. Why did I just nod? I talk! He blows smoke up into the air.

We walk along in silence and it's welcoming and peaceful. Surprisingly, it doesn't feel awkward. The street gets quieter as we get further away from college.

I take a chance and have a sneaky peak at Ryan. His dark brown hair suits him short; his icy blue eyes pierce out from behind his thick dark lashes and they crease at the corners when he smiles. His long muscular limbs match his six-foot-two-inches frame. He turns to me and smiles. Okay, so he definitely just caught me checking him out.

We reach the traffic lights at the top of my road.

"I just live down here." I point down my road. "Thanks for walking with me."

He drops his cigarette to the floor and twists his foot on it.

"I get it." He runs a hand over his short head. "You don't want anyone to see me walking you to your door. I understand."

"No, it's not that. I just live right at the other end of the street, at number 17. No point you walking down with me. I'm fine."

He stares at me for a second. Nervous, I instantly play with one of my braids. He looks at my hair, from the roots to the tips and smiles wider. What does that mean? Is my hair amusing?

"Okay, cool, I'll see you tomorrow." He rests a hand on my shoulder and holds my gaze for a moment too long. I can feel my nerves fizzing around my body bouncing off my skin.

He turns to walk away and I can't help but watch. There's something so effortlessly cool about Ryan. He's only two steps away when he stops.

"Hey, maybe you should give me your number? You know, in case you have another panic attack."

Cars stop at the red light next to us and they start forming a queue. I bet even the people in the cars are wondering what a guy like Ryan is doing talking to a girl like me.

"Pass me your phone."

I hand it over and he puts in his number.

"Text me or call me if you have another panic attack. I can talk you through it." He hands me back my phone. "See you tomorrow Amani."

I like the way he says my name. I look down at my phone in my hand with Ryan's number saved in it. I have Ryan's number! He starts to walk away again, this time lighting up another cigarette.

Out of habit, I go to message Sanaa and tell her that Ryan Bailey just gave me his number, as this is BIG news, but then I remember the argument and the reason I had a panic attack in the first place. The high I feel instantly deflates.

My phone vibrates in my hand and it's Mum.

"Sorry, one minute, I'm on our road," I say into the phone and start to run towards the house with my backpack banging against my back. And just like that, the feeling of panic creeps back.

TEN

"Hello?" I call out.

No answer.

"Mum? Grandad?"

"We're in the kitchen, Amani!" replies Mum.

I can tell from her tone that something is up. I kick my shoes off and drop my bag at the bottom of the stairs. I pop my head through the doorway into the living room looking for Grandad. His Motown records play quietly but he's not in there. I walk slowly towards the kitchen at the end of the corridor.

"Hurry up Marns, we're waiting."

I walk into the kitchen. Mum reaches out her hand and gently pulls me towards her. I follow her gaze across the table and stumble back. How is this even possible? Sitting opposite her is my dad.

It's been over a year since *that night* and now he's here. It's been ages since he's tried to speak to me. Why is he here? Has somebody died? Is he sick? Where is his car? Did I walk straight past it? Would I have even noticed it? Did he buy a new one? How did he get here? My brain is shooting so many questions that I can't even keep up.

The lighting in the kitchen is bright and unflattering, but

somehow Dad manages to look better than ever. His stubble is cut short, his hair is neat and low, and he's dressed in a sharp business suit. He doesn't look like the same man who used to take me to netball practice and call me 'Barmy Marni,' while throwing me over his shoulder. He definitely doesn't look like the same man who stood in the doorway in the rain on *that night* with his face swollen and angry.

He still has his coat on, which means he must have just arrived. Maybe he's not stopping long? There's a tension hovering in the room. It's crippling and makes the kitchen suddenly feel heavy and claustrophobic.

"Marns, sit down," Mum says, as she strokes my arm. She looks worn out and stressed and is wearing an old black jumper with pulls on it and a pair of washed-out, black work trousers.

I sit and Grandad puts a comforting hand on my knee, but it doesn't stop me from digging my fingernails into the palm of my hand. I can feel my chest getting tight again.

1 . . . 2 . . . 3 . . . 4.

No, it's not working. The brown table, Dad's brown coat. This is better. My brown skin, the brown door. . .

I breathe deep and slow. My breathing calms down slightly.

"Hi Marns." Finally, he speaks. "How are you?"

His voice makes me feel uneasy and nauseous. I swallow hard.

"Fine."

I don't want to ask him how he's doing. I just want to know why he's here. I want someone to tell me what the hell is going on. I look around the kitchen for a clue. A suitcase? A card? Some flowers? An explanation?

"Good." He pauses and looks down at the table. "Good,

I'm glad." He fiddles with his fingers. "Erm. . . well." Dad clears his throat.

"Oh, come on, Levi, don't you dare make me be the one to tell her!" Mum snaps, making me jump.

"Sorry, you're right. Amani, your mum asked me to come around." Mum huffs and shakes her head. "Sorry, I meant I wanted to come and tell you, face-to-face, that Zoe and I, well, me and Zoe, we're getting married."

Who the hell is Zoe?

"Zoe and I are getting married," Dad repeats trying to sound more upbeat but still refusing to make eye contact. "In December. And I—I mean, we, would like you to be a bridesmaid or at least part of the wedding in any way that you want to be. I want to be a part of your life again, Marns. I'm. . ." He tails off and attempts to smile at me.

I look at Mum and the corners of her eyes are watery and red. Grandad squeezes my hand and doesn't let go. What are they all expecting me to say? Does he really think he can turn up after all this time and tell me that he's getting married in a few months, to someone I don't know, and for me to do what exactly? Congratulate him? Who does he think he is showing up here and now deciding he wants a relationship with me!

Zoe? Zoe? I rack my brain. Was she the assistant from work? But I'm sure she was much younger than him. Did she have something to do with us leaving?

I look back at Dad and try to focus, realising I haven't answered his question. I don't want to be part of their wedding. I can see that Mum's legs are trembling under the table. I feel trapped. I need to leave. I need to lie down in my room away from everyone. If Mum knew why Dad was coming then she should have warned me.

"Amani?" Dad says. His eyes plead for me to speak.

No. He doesn't get to tell me what to do. That part of my life is over. I remain silent and my chest gets tighter. I can't breathe. I try to focus; I close my eyes. No, I need them open. I grab my chest hoping it will relieve the tightness but it doesn't.

"Are you okay? Take your time sweetie." Grandad says.

I look around frantically. Okay, there's yellow paint, yellow tiles, yellow tie. I feel like my mind is spinning. Where is it? I can't see anymore. I can feel my muscles twitching, willing me to stand up and escape, to run and leave this house and get as far away from him as possible.

"There's nothing else yellow!" I shout.

All three of them look at me with wide eyes.

I push the chair out from the table and it slams against the radiator. I hurry out of the kitchen, ignoring Mum asking me to come back.

"Yellow bag," I say under my breath as I pass my college bag in the hallway. I try to take a deep breath and finally my breathing starts to calm down.

I race up to my room and lay face down on my bed. Dad is marrying a woman that I've never even met. His life moved on after we left. Or did his life move on before we left? Does he treat Zoe the way he treated Mum? Is she scared of him?

I scream into my pillow and it helps. I just want him to go! I roll to my side and curl up into a ball. A single tear escapes from my eyes. I let it fall across my nose and down on to my bed.

I can hear mumbled talking downstairs and I wonder what

they're saying to each other. I can't believe they let him in the house. He's a monster. Have they forgotten what he did to us?

I look to the plant in the corner of my room. It looks how I feel—limp and lifeless. The amount of tears I want to cry right now would surely revive it, maybe even over-water it. My temples throb and there's a fuzzy ache at the back of my head that I haven't felt in a long time. I close my eyes to stop the tears from escaping and I keep my body still. I just concentrate on breathing and not crying. That's all I can focus on right now.

I'm gently being rocked. I wake up curled up on my bed with Mum next to me.

"What time is it?" My throat is dry and it comes out croaky.

"Almost eight. Did you have a nice sleep?"

Wow, I had no idea I had slept so long. I push myself up and lean back against the headboard. "Shouldn't you be at work?"

"I've called in sick, they can manage without me for one evening. You're more important. Here, your dad left this for you." She hands me a piece of paper with a number, an address and a date.

"Is that the wedding?"

Mum nods. "Just think about it. You don't have to do anything you don't want to do."

"I don't want to go."

"It's strange isn't it? Your dad getting re-married. But it seems to be important to him that you're involved." She leans over and wraps her body around mine. "No matter what has happened, he's still your dad."

I don't want to talk about him anymore so instead I snuggle into her and even as a teenager I still fit perfectly against her side like a jigsaw piece. A perfect fit. Just like it's always been.

ELEVEN

Life with Dad

"I think you've had enough to drink, Levi."

"I think I will decide when I've had enough!" Dad pours another large glass of whisky.

Mum sighs and walks out of the room, slamming the door behind her. Dad laughs. I cringe and try to tune him out by focusing on the TV.

"Why is your mum so uptight?" He nudges me, still laughing, trying to make me join in but I don't even look at him. "I'm talking to you. Don't be so rude." He tuts. "You're just like her sometimes."

I look at him and I can't help but feel sorry for him. My pity must show on my face because he suddenly throws his drink across the room leaving a pile of shattered glass on the carpet and a wet stain on the wall.

I scream at the noise and my heart races as the ringing of the smashed glass stings my eardrums. Dad's staring at me. His chest is rising and falling, his nostrils are flared and his fists are clenched.

Mum bursts back into the room taking in the scene and her eyes dart to me. I jump up to stand behind her.

"Go to your room, Amani. I don't want to look at you," Dad spits.

I run out of the room and I can hear Dad opening another drink.

TWELVE

I'm on my bed scrolling through my Instagram feed. I'm not even focusing on anything in particular, just stalling and trying to pass the time before I leave for college. I text Sanaa.

ME: *Hey, can we talk? x*

I send it, but I don't hold my breath for a reply; Sanaa can be really stubborn sometimes. I know if I told her my dad had turned up yesterday, she would reply instantly, but I don't feel ready to share that.

I throw my phone on the bed and sigh. If I'm going to make it to college on time I really need to move. My mind is willing me to stand up, but my body doesn't budge.

Mum pushes open my bedroom door. She looks even thinner than usual wrapped in her oversized, chunky cardigan. She slowly walks over to my bed and flops on to her back beside me. She lets out a sigh that matches mine.

I turn to face her.

"You too?" she says wiping a tear from my face.

I didn't even realise I was crying. She scoops me into her arms.

We lay on the bed hugging. I'm definitely late for college.

"One day off won't hurt," Mum says, reading my mind. She stands up and walks towards the door. "Marni." She pauses with her hand on the door handle. "I think you should call him today, before he goes back to London. He said he's staying in Manchester until Wednesday evening." She must see the confusion on my face. Why would she want me to call him? This is the man who nearly killed her. She pauses. "Just hear him out."

I open my mouth to respond but I don't have a chance before she leaves. Something tells me she wasn't waiting around for a response anyway.

My phone vibrates and I dart across the bed hoping it's Sanaa responding but it's Leo calling. He must have noticed I'm not in class. I really want to text him back but I don't know what to say. I can't tell him why I'm not in without telling him about my dad. I don't want to have that conversation with anyone.

I suddenly realise what Sanaa was saying about me not talking to her more. These are the types of things I should be discussing with my friends but I find it so hard to open up. I feel like I've kept the truth about my relationship with my parents a secret for so long that I can only share the watered-down version, which is that Dad was strict and controlling.

I know if I told Sanaa and Leo everything they would support me but what I don't want is their judgement or pity. I'm sure they would have questions too but even I don't understand why Dad treated us the way that he did. I've never told anyone about the day my dad hurt me, after Callum had walked me home. Not even Mum. I know it would destroy her and she's already been through so much.

I perch on the end of my bed staring down at my phone. Mum thinks I should call Dad. I don't really want to but I know she will ask me about it again later.

Let's just get this over and done with.

I grab the note from beside my bed and dial the number before I have the chance to talk myself out of it. With each ring I lose a little bit of faith that he'll answer his phone. As I'm about to give up, he picks up.

"Hello? Marns is that you?"

I take a deep breath. "Hi Dad." I hear the wobble in my voice. Even just saying his name leaves me with a bitter aftertaste.

"Marni, baby girl, I'm so glad that you called, but shouldn't you be in college?"

"I have a free morning," I lie, not that I need to explain myself to him.

"I see. How's college? What are you studying? Do you like it in Manchester?" he reels off question after question like he's interviewing me for a magazine.

I feel like telling him to "quit the small talk" but I'm not feeling that ballsy.

"College is fine. Everyone here's pretty nice. I've got two best friends called Sanaa and Leo." I wince as I say their names, feeling guilty for not acting like much of a friend lately. I wonder if Dad will say anything about me having a boy as a friend? But he doesn't. I'm sure he would have something to say if he saw all six-foot of Leo. "I'm studying Sociology, English and Media. I'm still hoping to be a journalist one day."

"That's amazing Marni! Do you still play netball?"

"No, not anymore."

"Oh that's a shame, you always were the best on the team."

I can hear him smiling as he speaks. He always used to tell everyone that I was the star of the team. He would even argue with my coach in school. It worked because it got me on to the A-Team, but then he stopped coming to my matches. He was always working too late or at least that's what he said.

"So, you're enjoying life here with your mum and Grandad?"

"Yeah, I like it a lot. It's calmer and I'm settled." The other end of the phone falls quiet. "Dad?"

"I'm still here. Sorry, was just thinking that you sound happy. Your mum is doing a great job with you and you both are clearly thriving."

I shake my head erasing the thoughts of Mum in bed refusing to get up, not eating a proper meal for days on end, spending all her time working or asleep. She's been doing okay the past few days but it's so up and down. I know she's trying hard to hold it all together for me.

"Mum's the best," I say. I feel my heart swell with loyalty for her.

He doesn't respond and I don't speak, so we sit in an awkward silence. I wonder what he's thinking. To be honest I don't even know what I'm thinking.

"So, Marni." He hesitates for a moment. "Like I was saying yesterday, Zoe and I would really like you to be part of our wedding. What do you think? It would be great if you could come to London and meet her. I think you two would really get along."

I bite my lip to stop myself from scoffing.

"We have this apartment in North London and you would love it," Dad continues. "It's modern and we have two bedrooms so you can come and stay."

I don't want to be part of his new life with his new wife and new apartment. Has he totally forgotten what he put me through? And what about Mum? How is she going to feel if I were to start flaunting Dad's new life in front of her?

"Marns, are you still there?"

"Yeah, sorry. I'm not sure Dad. Can you give me some time to think?"

"Yes, of course."

"Thanks, I'll call you soon."

"Okay. I love you, Marni."

I pause for a moment. I can't remember the last time he said that to me.

"Bye Dad." I hang up the phone.

I hadn't realised how badly my hands are shaking. I ball them into fists to stop them. That was much harder than I thought but I didn't give in to what he wanted. He can't control me anymore.

THIRTEEN

Life with Dad

"I'm going to be working away for a few days, Marns."
I stop typing and turn to face Dad as he gets comfortable on the end of my bed. I'm trying so hard to not to let the excitement show on my face.

"Do you think you can look after your mum while I'm away?"

I nod and fight the urge to explain to him that she doesn't need looking after when he's not here. The only time that she's in danger is when he has his hands wrapped around her throat or he's thrown her to the ground.

I love it when Dad's working away. I know that I'm not going to wake up to the sound of screaming. And Mum is completely different when it's just me and her. She lets my friends stay over, she messes around with makeup and we don't even mention Dad's name. Not once!

It feels like there's never enough time because before we know it Dad's back bringing a dark cloud with him and the house feels like it's shrinking and suffocating. Mum and I try to make ourselves as small as possible praying that this time things will be different. That he won't notice we're there.

FOURTEEN

Last night I dreamt about Dad and Zoe in a church. Zoe (who had no face or features, probably because I've never actually seen her) was in a white dress and all of our friends and family were there. I was in a bridesmaid dress walking down the aisle behind Zoe.

The dream was confusing because I felt happy for Dad and Zoe like I was almost excited to be there. Then when we reached the alter, I looked up at Dad standing next to Zoe, and he leaned over and kissed me on the cheek. Then I woke up.

This is the first time since meeting them last summer that I haven't seen or spoken to Sanaa in over 48 hours. I miss her but she still hasn't responded to my text.

I waste time, lazing around, scrolling through everyone's Instagram stories. I come across Leo's and I see Ryan looking cute in the background. They're at football practice and Leo and one of his teammates are clowning around.

I search Leo's friend list for Ryan's profile. I find him, but his account is private. His profile picture is topless. A smile creeps across my face as I try to zoom in. Damn, he looks good.

I look at Sanaa's profile next and she hasn't posted since our argument. I start to type her a message.

ME: *Hey San*

Delete.

ME: *I'm really sorry about what I said*

Delete.

ME: *U ok?*

Delete.

ME: *I miss you*

I press send and head downstairs. Mum's sitting alone watching TV but I notice that her eyes are puffy and red.

"You okay?"

"Hey, oh, I thought you were at college. You off today?" Mum rubs at her eyes but it ends up looking worse. She pats the cushion next to her.

"I'm going in later." I sit next to her. "I called Dad yesterday."

She smiles. "I'm proud of you. Was it all okay?"

I nod.

Mum uses her thumb to stroke circles on my face. It's so comforting, and only then do I realise that I've been craving her touch for a long time. I've needed her attention so desperately but she's been so busy and tired and sad.

"Shouldn't you be at work?"

I feel Mum stiffen. I instantly regret it as she pulls her hand away.

"I swapped shifts," she says quickly.

My phone vibrates. I quickly look at it hoping it's Sanaa but it's a message from Leo.

"Everything okay?"

"Yeah," I say as I read the messages. "It's Leo."

I glance at Mum and she is peering down at my phone. I quickly tilt it away from her and she laughs. My phone pings. Two kisses from Leo.

"You know two means something," Mum says and she winks at me.

We both burst out laughing and I feel like I haven't laughed in so long. But, as usual, that lightness quickly disappears and my head is buzzing with questions and what-ifs.

"Mum, can I ask you something? Was Dad seeing Zoe before we left? Is that why we left or was it the arguments and—" I stop abruptly because I just can't quite bring myself to say 'abuse.'

Mum inhales and that look of dread comes back to her face like it never left.

"Sorry," I quickly say. I shouldn't have brought it up.

"Don't apologise, Amani. None of this is your fault. Me and your dad weren't meant to work. I wish we were more compatible. Do you remember when I got pregnant?"

I nod.

"Well, I found out about Zoe and your dad while I was pregnant. It was a total shock, I didn't suspect a thing, but in the end all the stress caused me to lose the baby." She pauses and swallows hard, fighting back the tears. "When your dad found out about the miscarriage, he found it very hard to deal with. He blamed me. He got into his head that I had purposely lost the baby. Even accused me of pushing him to cheat. He was acting like a crazy person." Mum shakes her head. "I know grief hits everyone differently but he was wrong to put that on me. Anyway, he reassured me it was over with Zoe and I believed him. But your dad was still so angry. He refused to go to counselling and he took it all out on me." She looks up to the ceiling, bravely fighting back the tears. "The abuse got worse after I lost the baby. In the end there was no more trust, respect or love."

She brushes away a tear that's rolling down her face. I wrap my arms around her and she sinks into me. I rub her back and stroke her hair like I'm the mother and she's my baby.

"You know, I think you're really strong for leaving him."

"Thank you," Mum whispers.

"Why did you never go to the police? That time I called them—you sent them away—I never understood why."

"I was scared that they wouldn't believe me and honestly I was scared of your dad. He said he would take you away if I ever told anyone and I knew he would. But Marni even though I'm still working through stuff with your dad, I can see that he's different. He's calmer, he seems more aware of what he's saying and at the end of the day he's still your dad and he loves you even if we're not together anymore."

Does he? It's easy to say you love someone but actions speak louder. I need time to see if my dad has really changed.

"I'll make some tea. Tea makes everything better, doesn't it?" I say and Mum smiles. The tears have dried up.

"Yes, please."

As I wait for the kettle to boil, I think about what Mum said. If I was her would I have stayed? Has Zoe seen the monster that lives in Dad and is scared to leave too? God knows I will never be with a man like my dad. Ever!

I pour the tea into two mugs and put some biscuits on a plate. As I turn to leave the kitchen, I notice a leaflet poking out of Mum's bag. I pick it up and my heart sinks as I read it: 'So, you're depressed: how to cope.'

I don't mention anything to Mum as I hand her the tea but as soon as I get to my room, I Google depression and Mum definitely has a lot of the symptoms. I knew that Mum's behaviour was concerning with all the sleeping and not eating but depression! Has she been to the doctor? Does she need medication? Does Grandad know? It seems cruel that Dad is getting married and Mum is in such a dark place.

"Marns, yuh okay?" Grandad comes into my room. He rests his hand on my shoulder.

"Hey Grandad, have you spoken to Mum? She's really upset today."

He nods. "I spoke to her yesterday."

"So, what do we do?"

"Yuh mama is gon be fine. She is gon bounce back, like always."

"I think she needs to see a doctor," I say slowly. "For her depression."

Grandad tuts in response. "She jus tired. She work too hard."

"But Grandad—"

Grandad puts his hand up to silence me. "Yuh may not wan my advice and yuh can choose to tek it or leave it, but I tink that yuh should speak to 'im. It will help yuh heal."

I frown. "Who are you talking about?"

"Yuh dad. Now I know tings have 'appened in the past wit 'im and yuh mum. I know words 'ave been said and unfortunately tings got out of 'and, but if I can let that man in to my 'ouse after what 'im did to my daughter, I tink you should find it somewhere in yuh heart to listen to 'im. Yuh mother will not stop lovin' yuh no matter what yuh decide, yuh understand?"

I nod and Grandad kisses me on the forehead before he leaves. My head is buzzing and I massage my forehead. Since I moved here my life has been calm but why does it feel like everything is spiralling out of control?

Later that day I summon the courage to send a text to Dad asking to meet him and Zoe. Maybe Mum and Grandad are right? Maybe he has changed? Maybe I do need to do this to help me get over what happened?

As soon as I press send my stomach twists and knots. I wonder how he'll react when he gets my message? Will he be angry because I haven't mentioned the bridesmaid question? My phone buzzes almost immediately.

DAD: *Great news! We can't wait. I will send you some money for a ticket to London xxx*

FIFTEEN

Life with Dad

I gently tap on the door to Dad's office at home and wait for a response. Despite walking past this door every single day I've only been in a handful of times.

"What?" he barks.

I open the door and he's sat at his desk, the computer screen reflecting in his reading glasses.

He's still in his shirt from work but he's taken off his tie and undone a few of his top buttons. He doesn't look up and I hover in the doorway.

I want to turn around and run back upstairs but I don't. I wait for him to finish typing. Eventually, he looks at me, pulling his glasses off his face.

"Baby girl." He grins. "You okay?"

I nod and take a seat on one of the comfy seats beside his desk.

"Have you come to stop your daddy from working so hard?"

I smile, feeling awkward. I was actually there to ask him what happened to Mum's arm and to tell him to leave if he didn't love her anymore. But now that I'm here I don't feel so brave. I swallow hard.

"What's on your mind?"

"Mum and you." I drop my gaze and fumble with my braids.

"What about her?" he spits.

"Is everything okay with you two? Because it doesn't really feel like it."

He frowns at me. "She told you to ask me this?"

"No! She doesn't even know I'm here."

He scratches his head. I place my palms flat on the chair by my sides ready to run if he gets angry. He's so unpredictable nowadays that I feel on edge just sitting beside him.

"I don't think your mum would be happy to know that you're prying and asking me questions." He stands up and opens the door. "And I don't think you should mention this again, Amani. Do you understand?"

"But—"

"You can go."

I nod and stand up to leave the room, disappointed in myself for not being braver.

SIXTEEN

I drag myself out of bed and get ready for college. I pull on some ripped jeans and a black slogan t-shirt that says, 'Girl Gang.' Sanaa and I both have matching ones.

I check my phone to see if she's text me this morning. Nothing. I check her Instagram and she's uploaded one new photo of four amethyst crystal necklaces on a white silk cloth. I can actually imagine her with her mum's silk blouse on the floor laying them out and trying to get that perfect shot. The caption reads 'Perfect matching necklaces for you and your Girl Gang.'

I look down at my top and sigh. I've not felt this lonely in a long time. She posted it last night and it already had 9728 likes and 627 comments. I doubt she feels lonely.

I grab my jacket and make my way downstairs. The smell of cornmeal porridge and cinnamon fill the house and my stomach grumbles. I love it when Grandad gets up early and makes porridge. I can hear his Beres Hammond record playing quietly in the living room.

There are voices coming from the kitchen and I check my watch. Mum's normally at work by now, so who is Grandad talking to? I make my way into the kitchen and push open the door to see Grandad and Leo eating porridge and playing cards.

"Hi." I look from Leo to Grandad and back again. "What are you doing here?"

"I came to walk with you," Leo says easily, like I haven't been ignoring him. "I tried to call you, but you never got back, so I just thought I would come and see you. Plus, cornmeal porridge, you know, I can't resist." He grins.

I move over to the counter and grab a bowl, as they continue their game of Blackjack.

"I wasn't ignoring you. I was just. . ." I trail off lamely.

"Busy?" Leo says, raising his eyebrows.

"Yeah, just busy." I sit down at the table and focus on eating so I don't have to look at Leo.

"So, Leo, university?" Grandad asks while studying his cards "Marni, tells me yuh tinkin' of going to do football?"

Leo leans back in his chair. "That's the plan. I just need to talk to my parents about it and hopefully I'll get scouted." He confidently shares his plans for the future with Grandad and I'm confused about why he can't just do that with his own parents.

"Well, as a parent 'n' grandparent." Grandad stresses the 't' as he pats me on the arm proudly. "I tink, yuh parents will be 'appy as long as you are. Dey will jus' wan' yuh to be 'appy n safe."

Leo nods in agreement, just as the doorbell rings and Grandad gets up to answer it.

"Are you mad that I turned up here?" Leo asks once Grandad is out of earshot.

"No, it's cool. We're cool."

"Amani?" Grandad pushes open the kitchen door. "Dere's anudda bwoi here f'yuh. He said he's walking wit you dis morning." Grandad winks at me and standing behind him is Ryan.

Ryan Bailey. Is. In. My. House.

Leo frowns and looks from me to Ryan and back again.

"Hey." Ryan smiles.

I wish I had put more thought into my outfit this morning.

Leo stands up and pats him on the back. "Ryan, what you doing here, mate?"

"Hey bro, didn't see you there."

They touch fists but I can feel the tension. Grandad must sense it too because he quickly sits at the table and watches them, amused.

"I just hadn't heard from Amani or seen her around college," Ryan explains. "So I came to check on her."

He looks at me. Wait, was I actually supposed to contact him? Had he been waiting for my text?

"You?"

Leo glances at me. "Yeah, same."

Now they're both waiting for me to say something and I don't know what to say.

"We'll have to finish this game another time, Leo," Grandad says saving me. "Unlucky that you've got to go. I was going to let you win this morning as well."

Leo laughs. "Thanks for breakfast."

"Shall we go?" I say and Leo and Ryan look at each other.

"Sure," Ryan says easily, but Leo is sending me death stares.

"See you later, Grandad, love you." I practically run out of the kitchen, grabbing my bag and jacket as I unlock the door all in one smooth movement.

With both boys outside away from Grandad's amused prying eyes, I feel slightly less stressed. *Slightly.*

"Amani—"

"Marns, I—"

They both talk to me at the same time.

This is going to be a long walk.

It feels good to be out and about. I feel like I've been cooped up for days. The changes in the colour of the leaves seems to have happened overnight. They look like golden, orange halos. I love this time of year.

"So, how've you been? Any—"

"I'm good thanks." I cut him off not wanting to mention the panic attack in front of Leo.

We walk along the street beside the park, the same street we walked down on Monday when he gave me his number. I smile at the memory. A lot has happened since then. Leo gets distracted by something on his phone and falls behind so I take my chance.

"Have you missed me?" I ask bravely. Hoping it comes across flirty and not just weird.

A smile creeps across Ryan's face. "Yeah, but you obviously didn't miss me! I was waiting for you to call or text." He tilts his head as though waiting for some sort of explanation. "I've been waiting by the phone, Marni." He pokes his bottom lip out for effect.

He's been waiting by the phone!

"Yeah, well, you said to text or call you *if* I had another panic attack and needed you, so I didn't think I was allowed."

Ryan stops walking and dramatically places his hand on his chest. "Oh, shots fired! Okay, you want to be clever? Let me make it clear—you should text me or call me when you *want* me." And he flashes me a classic Ryan smile with perfect teeth, that one dimple. Why is this boy so fine?

"Cool," I say and the butterflies in my stomach take flight.

"You should come and watch me after school at football practice, we could go to Fabio's after?"

"Amani doesn't watch football," Leo yells.

I glare at him and he smiles back.

"It's not like I don't want to," I say carefully. "But I can't today. I'm helping my grandad with dinner."

"Tomorrow then?"

"Maybe." I can feel Leo watching me. "I can come and watch you both."

I'm relieved when we get to the bus stop outside college and the street is swarming with college kids. I slow down as we pass the bus stop to see if I can see Sanaa. I can't and my heart sinks. I can't see her by the college steps either.

"So?" Ryan touches the sleeve on my jacket.

"Sorry, what?"

Leo's staring at Ryan's hand touching me. I subtly move away so Ryan's hand falls.

"I said Jessica is having a party on Saturday and I wondered if you wanted to come with me?"

"Err." I make the mistake of looking at Leo who's subtly shaking his head. *Why?*

The steps are becoming more crowded as students run to their first class.

"Let me think about it? I've gotta run to class." I wave goodbye as I hurry up the steps.

"Yeah, cool, text me," Ryan shouts after me and I grin.

Ryan Bailey just asked me out on a date!

I head to our normal lunch spot at the back of the canteen to wait for Sanaa. From there I have a good view of the whole room. I just want to work things out. It's ironic she felt like I didn't tell her enough about my life, and now here I am desperate to tell her everything.

It's been 10 minutes and there's no sign of her. A group of girls are hovering nearby, waiting for the table. I grab my bag and stand up to leave. There's no point keeping the table just for myself but then Leo spots me and waves so I sit back down, ignoring the annoyed glances the girls throw my way.

Leo makes his way through the crowds towards me, twisting left and right and skimming past rowdy groups, saying "Hi" to a few as he passes.

"Hey." He sits down and takes the two boxes of cheesy chips off the tray and places one in front of himself and one in front of me, then does the same with the two drinks.

"You got me lunch? Thank you."

Leo shrugs like it's nothing.

I place a cheesy chip in my mouth. So good! I'd never had cheesy chips before moving to Manchester, and in the first few weeks I couldn't get enough of them. Southerners are really losing out by not embracing this. I shove more in my mouth and Leo watches me amused.

"Good to see you've not lost your appetite then."

"Never," I reply. "Have you seen Sanaa?" Leo shakes his head. "Is she okay?"

He shrugs. "Sanaa's Sanaa."

Sometimes I wish Leo was a girl.

"I'm more bothered about you though," he continues. "Talk to me."

"I don't know where to start. Sanaa and I said loads of hurtful things that we didn't mean and we haven't spoken since. I messaged her, but she aired me and I don't know what to do."

"What kind of hurtful things?"

"She said my mum was depressed," I say. "And that I was going the same way, but I'm not though. I said she was a bad friend and never listens."

"Do you think your mum's depressed?" Leo asks gently.

I think back to the leaflet that I found in her bag. "I mean, I didn't, but lately she's been so low. I don't know what to do or how to help her."

"What did your Grandad say?"

I roll my eyes. "He thinks she's just tired."

"Was it your dad's visit that's made your mum worse?"

"How do you know about that?" I snap. I instantly feel my body stiffen.

"Your Grandad told me this morning, sorry."

"He did?"

Grandad's not the most open person in the world, so I'm surprised.

"Nobody expects you to be able to deal with this on your own, Amani. It's a lot to take in." He waits a beat. "You know I'm here for you. Don't push me away."

I smile at him. "You're a good friend and I promise to do better myself."

Leo chews on his bottom lips and I can just tell he has something else to say.

"So." He stabs aimlessly with his fork, avoiding eye contact. "Ryan Bailey, huh? What's up with that?" He's trying to sound nonchalant, but I can hear in his voice that he's not cool with it.

"I'm not sure," I reply honestly. "Nothing really. We spoke after my argument with Sanaa and just kind of clicked."

"Are you going to Jessica's party with him this weekend?"

"I'm not sure if I'm in the party mood."

There's a strange tension between us. Is he angry at me? Or Ryan? Or am I just imagining things?

We reach for the tissues in the middle of the table at the same time and our hands brush. It feels like electricity is bolting through my veins. Leo's staring at his hand and I'm sure he felt it too.

The bell goes and we both jump and suddenly it's like the spell is broken.

"Alright, well, let me know about the party," Leo says.

"I owe you one." I pick up our rubbish. "Tomorrow I'll buy you lunch and you can fill me in on your life." He smiles and I instantly feel better.

"Looking forward to it."

SEVENTEEN

That evening, I push my dinner around my plate. I can't stop thinking about my conversation with Leo. I hate the thought of him thinking that I push people away. I really don't want to, but it's so hard to be an open book when there are some chapters I want to forget.

Grandad puts his fork down and stops eating. Mum's at work so it's just me and him tonight. It's been nice having Mum around for the past few evenings, but I know she needed to be back at work. I just wish I had caught her before her shift to see for myself how she is.

"Amani, yuh gonna eat your chicken or just play wit it? I made yuh favourite and yuh not even eating it."

He's right—brown stew chicken with rice and peas is my favourite but right now I just can't stomach it.

I smile and put some food in my mouth to show I'm making an effort.

"Is dis about dem bwoi?" he continues.

I groan. I really do *not* want to have this conversation with him.

"Leo and 'im friend," he says just to make his point clear. "I've always told yuh Amani, yuh are x-actly like yuh Grandmother—da way yuh carry yo'self. Yuh 'ave no idea how *beautiful* you really are, it was only a matta of time before yuh had bwoi fighting over yuh."

"It's not like that. Leo is a friend and Ryan—" *What is Ryan?* "Well, I don't know," I admit.

"Me ah never look pon my 'fren' like dat! That bwoi there wants more than just a frenship." He raises his eyebrows knowingly. "An you'd be chupid not to act. Leo's good! As wit the other one, me nah know him, yuh like 'im?"

"Ryan just saw me upset at college and has been checking in on me ever since. I suppose he just wants to make sure I'm alright."

He knowingly raises his eyebrow again and I know exactly what he means. "Upset?"

"I'm fine."

Neither of us believe what I'm saying. I force myself to eat so Grandad won't question me further.

After dinner I'm supposed to be doing my homework but I end up just laying on my bed, staring at the ceiling. Maybe going to the party isn't a bad idea. What else am I going to do? And getting to spend time with Ryan is something I can't resist.

ME: *Hey. Soz about running off 2day. I've been thinking and yeah we should go to Jessica's party.*

I bite my nails and wait for Ryan to text me back. My phone pings a minute later.

RYAN: *Finally, she txts me!!! I think we should go to the party together too.*

Yes, yes, yes! I start to type back but another text comes through.

RYAN: *Glad u didn't leave me hanging for too long though. Was beginning 2 feel stupid.*

He was beginning to feel stupid! Stupid, because of me? My heart skips a beat as I delete what I was going to say and type a new message.

ME: *Sorry. I just needed to think.*

RYAN: *About Leo?*

Yes, sort of.

ME: *No!!! There's nothing going on with Leo!*

Too defensive. Delete. I settle with a question mark.

RYAN: *You thinking about how to let him down gently?*

Wait is Ryan jealous?

ME: *I'm not letting him down. Leo and I are friends, we're cool.*

RYAN: *He knows that?*

I read the message over and over again. I'm not sure what to reply. It's not like Leo has told me that he wants to be more than friends. What am I thinking? Of course he doesn't want to be more than friends.

ME: *Yeah, we're cool.*

RYAN: *Cool. that's fine then. I just don't like to share ;) Wanna go Fabio's? I can meet you after football – one day you'll come watch me. I can feel it.*

A date? I have a date with Ryan! Okay be cool Amani.

ME: *Sounds good x*

RYAN: *See you tomorrow x*

He sent me a kiss! I cover my face with my pillow and let out a squeal of excitement. A thought flashes through my head: maybe not having Sanaa around has allowed people to actually see me for once and do you know what? I really like it.

EIGHTEEN

Leo is sat waiting at our table in the canteen. He doesn't notice me approaching as he's busy on his phone. I scan the hall for Ryan and Sanaa but can't see either of them. As I get within earshot I point to the boxes of chips and drinks already on the table.

"Hey, today was supposed to be my treat."

"Don't worry, I got out of class a little early and the queues were quiet. You can owe me one." He slips his phone in to his pocket as I put my backpack on the seat beside me and sit down.

"Where's Sanaa?" I ask.

"She's got a cold so she's not in today." Leo shoves a handful of chips into his mouth. "Her and her mum came round for dinner last night and she seemed fine. I bet she's faking or something to avoid a test."

"You didn't tell her did you? About my dad?"

"No way! I wouldn't do that, but have you spoken to him?"

"Not much, I'm still processing the fact he's getting married again."

Leo almost chokes on his chips. "For real? When?"

"December. He wants me to be a bridesmaid but I don't think I can."

"Why? You don't like who he's marrying?"

I suddenly feel hot and take a long sip of my drink. Leo watches me patiently.

"My dad. . . he did some pretty messed up things." I swallow and the words seem stuck in my throat but I want to tell him. "He used to hit my mum. I saw it all and that's why we left."

Leo's eyes bulge. "Are you serious?"

"We're still dealing with the after-effects of it and Mum isn't coping well."

"Marni, I'm so sorry. I had no idea."

"It's fine, how would you? It's just hard to talk about, you know?"

"Maybe you need closure, so you can move on? Have you ever spoken to him about it all?"

"No, I'm going to see him soon but you're right, I want him to explain why he did the things he did. Maybe then I can forgive him."

Truthfully, I'm scared to confront my dad. He would kick off over the slightest things so how was he going to react to me questioning him?

By the time I arrive at Fabio's after college most of Kemble College are already swarming the place. I stop when I spot Sanaa who clearly isn't sick and she's sitting at our booth with Morgan and Alicia. We're pretty much only on 'hi' terms with them so how did they get so close?

Ryan's waiting for me on the table behind Sanaa's. If she can move on and get new friends then so can I, but as I get nearer to Sanaa, I feel my palms getting sweaty. She spots me but it's like she doesn't see me. She looks right through me as though I don't even exist. I've seen her do it to people before but to be on the receiving end of it hurts.

Ryan stands up as I approach our table and flings his arms around me. He kisses me on the top of my head, and pulls me in the booth with him. He smells of smoke and aftershave.

"Did you see Ryan kiss her?" I hear Morgan say to Sanaa.

"Thought you were gonna stand me up." He playfully strokes my arm.

"As if, you practically begged me to come," I tease, while checking my makeup in my compact mirror. I would never normally do that but something about meeting Ryan after school had me rushing to the bathroom during last period and trying my best to give myself a winged eye-liner and now I'm conscious it's smudged.

"You look great!" he says, playfully knocking the mirror out of my hand. He looks at my face for a few moments then his eyes drift to my braids. "Do you ever do other styles with your hair?"

I scoff, hoping he's joking, but as he lifts the ends of one of my braids, I see he's serious.

"What do you mean?" I ask slowly.

"Well, it's just always down and in these." He's furrowing his brow as he twiddles the braid between his thumb and forefinger. I want to knock it out of his hand, but I don't.

"I can do other things with it. I just like it like this." I pull away, feeling uncomfortable. "Would you prefer a huge Afro?"

Ryan bites his lip and leans back as though imagining me with an Afro. "No, keep those then." He turns to look at the menu.

I fiddle with my braids. *I like my hair like this. Is something wrong with it?*

"I'm starving!" Ryan says, flicking through the menu. "What you gonna get? I'm thinking to try this protein Snickers shake." He points at one of the milkshakes in the 'Lite Shakes and Gym Buddies' section of the menu.

Me, Leo and Sanaa usually laugh at that section. I mean who comes for a milkshake if they're watching their weight?

"Cool, I'll have an Oreo milkshake," I say without even checking the menu.

"Cool." He nods "I'll get you skimmed milk."

"I like it with whole milk."

"Yeah, but you gotta keep that figure right for me innit." He stands up and winks at me before he walks off to the till.

I look down at my stomach slightly rolled over my waist band. I suck it in and sit up straight.

I watch Ryan at the till and he's talking to a tall, leggy blonde girl. She's laughing and flicking her hair around. Why is her hand on his arm? I fight the urge to get up and walk over. She strokes his arm and whispers in his ear and Ryan makes no attempt to push her away. I glance over at Sanaa's table and they're deep in a conversation so they thankfully haven't noticed.

Am I overreacting? We aren't exclusive or anything so he can talk to girls. But I can't help but think if I was acting like that with Leo he would be pissed.

"What are you gonna wear tomorrow?" I overhear Morgan ask.

"I've got a leopard print dress; it's fitted and has a shimmer to it. I'm thinking that with boots. So, it's not too dressy, you know? What about you?" I hear Sanaa reply and I know exactly which dress she means.

"Oh Sanaa, you look good in anything," coos Morgan. "I don't know what to wear. I can never decide."

"Well, you can come to mine before we go? Borrow whatever you like. You too, Alicia."

Her wardrobe used to be my wardrobe. What the hell am I going to wear tomorrow?

"I knew you were faking it," I hear Leo's voice and I put my menu up so it blocks my face. I don't want him to see me with Ryan.

"You totally believed me." Sanaa laughs.

"You seen Amani?"

"Yeah she's here with Ryan."

"Ryan?"

"Yeah over there."

Someone taps on my menu and I lower it bracing myself for Leo but it's Ryan with a grin on his face and two milkshakes.

Leo and Sanaa are staring at me. Leo shakes his head and walks away and Sanaa tuts and turns back to her new friends. I want to call out to him but I don't know what to say.

Ryan sips from his milkshake. "What's Leo doing here?"

"He must have come to see Sanaa," I lie.

I drink from my milkshake but it doesn't hit the same way it usually does. I can feel Ryan watching me but thankfully he doesn't bring Leo up again.

When I arrive home it's nearing six and Grandad is in the

kitchen cooking. Mum's working late tonight and the table is already laid out for the both of us.

"Sumtin' arrived for yuh today Amani, it's in here." He points at a box on the chair opposite me. "I guessed it was probably from yuh dad so I put it out of sight fo' now. Away from yuh mum, you know?"

I nod knowing exactly what he means.

I look down at the box on the table and it's neatly wrapped in parchment paper. It's got my name and address printed neatly on the top. I use my house key to score the Sellotape and peel back the parchment. I lift off the lid and there's something wrapped in green tissue paper. I take it out to unwrap it and it is a small golden hair clip. It has a green gemstone and it looks expensive. There's a note underneath it.

Dear Amani,
I would be so honoured if you would be a bridesmaid at our wedding. Here's one of the hair clips that all of the bridesmaids will wear on the big day. I hope you like it. I have included some ideas for bridesmaids dresses in the box. Let me know which one you like the most. I look forward to meeting you soon.
Zoe xx

I read the note again before looking in the bottom of the box and see torn-out pictures from bridal magazines. She's circled a range of bridesmaid dresses and there's a stunning forest green one that catches my eye. In fact, they're all quite nice. I look back at the hair clip and fumble with it between my fingers. I can feel Grandad watching me. I look at him and he raises his eyebrows. I put the hair clip back into the box.

"Why have they sent that? I haven't even said I'm going to the wedding."

"Maybe 'im sent it as token gesture, olive branch, who knows. But yuh no 'ave to do anytin wit it."

Grandad makes it sound so easy but I can't help but wonder if Dad put Zoe up to this. If Dad wants me to be part of the wedding, I'm sure he'll do anything he can to make it happen. I glare at the box. This time he won't get his way.

NINETEEN

Where is he? I arrive to the party on time and Ryan is nowhere to be seen and he's not picking up his phone. I stare at my mobile frustrated. I made an effort tonight—hair in a bun, glittery crop top, tight jeans, new shoes, and for what?

It's freezing outside so I go in, taking off my coat at the same time. I push my way through the crowd to the kitchen. I find some Jack Daniels and mix it with some lemonade in a plastic cup and down it quickly. I pour another.

"Here she is!" It's Leo and he has his arm around Morgan, one of Sanaa's new friends.

I can't hide my surprise. Is Sanaa okay with Morgan hanging around Leo? I've never even seen them talk.

"Drinking alone?" Leo asks but before I can answer Morgan whispers something in his ear. Seeing her lips that close to him makes me feel weird.

"Your boyfriend's out in the back garden, if you're looking for him." Morgan flashes me a fake smile.

I don't bother responding. In the back garden there are even more people. I can't see Ryan anywhere. I bet Morgan's just sent me here to make me look stupid. Just as I'm about to give up I spot him at the far end of the garden. I walk towards him and realise he's not alone.

They break away when they see me and she quickly scarpers past me and back into the house. It's the blonde girl from Fabio's. Were they kissing? I'm not sure but I'm pissed.

"There you are." Ryan puts his arms out like he wants me to run into them.

I don't move, instead I look him up and down. "What was that about?"

Ryan frown and shrugs. "That girl? It was nothing."

"It didn't look like nothing."

"Let's not fight babe." He bites his lip as he checks me out. "You look sexy. I really like your hair like that."

I can't help but smile and feel glad that he noticed that I did my hair different.

He swigs on his beer and lights up a cigarette. He offers me a drag and I put the cigarette to my lips and inhale. Ryan smiles like a proud parent. I hold the smoke in my mouth and throat for a moment and then blow it out. I run my tongue along the roof of my mouth and try not to gag.

"First time?" I nod. "You did good."

He's looking at me like I'm the most delicious thing he's ever seen. I can see girls sneakily looking over at us. Ryan takes the cigarette back off me, takes one last drag before throwing it on the floor.

"Come on, let's get a drink, beautiful." He interlocks his fingers with mine and we go into the kitchen.

Leo's still in the kitchen but now he's talking to another girl called Dani, a tall, mixed-raced girl with curly hair. I squeeze past and reach for the JD.

"Your hair's different." Leo says to me.

"Just trying something new."

97

"Oh, of course you're here bothering her. Why am I not surprised?" Ryan throws his arm around my exposed waist.

"Whatever," Leo says. He grabs Dani's hand and walks out of the kitchen.

I hand Ryan his drink and we cheers and down them straight away. The alcohol instantly hits me.

"One more." Ryan hands me another and I push it away. He pouts. "Please, for me?"

I know I shouldn't but I don't want him to think I'm no fun.

"Last one," I say and he nods. I quickly drink it and squeeze my eyes shut as it burns my throat.

He throws his drink back and slams the empty cup on the counter. "Come on."

He pulls me back through the crowd and into the living room. It's crowded and people are dancing and grinding on each other. Ryan takes me to the corner where his friends are.

"Here, join them, I'll be one minute." Ryan points to the sofa and a sea of white girls look up from their phones and stare at me. I turn to look at Ryan for support but he's already in the corner having a laugh with his friends.

"I'm Chloe," one of the girls say. "I'm here with Luke Owens."

"Amani," I reply. "I came with Ryan Bailey."

"Yeah, we saw." Chloe looks at me amused. "You guys serious?"

I shrug. "It's early days."

"You're not really Ryan's type."

I don't know if it's the alcohol making me brave but I lean in and say, "And what type is that?"

The girl jerks her head back and the others stare at me.

I know exactly what she means and I want her to say it but instead she turns away and one by one the girls angle their bodies so I'm shut out.

I look around the room. Everyone looks like they're having a good time. I thought coming to a party with Ryan would make me feel good, special even. Now I wish I was back at home.

I spot Sanaa in the far corner of the room with Tyler Baxter. Their eyes are locked as they dance together. Ryan's still joking around with his friends not paying any attention to me.

I miss her.

I feel my eyes watering and I quickly wipe them hoping no one saw. What am I even doing here? I stand up and I feel unsteady on my feet. I stumble out of the living room, bumping into people as I make my way out of the front door. I put on my coat as I step out of the front gate and immediately see Leo with Dani kissing and that's when I throw up all over my new shoes.

TWENTY

I'm dreaming that I'm in a car with Ryan. He's telling me I'm not good enough for him. He keeps shouting that I'm useless. I don't respond, but my hurt is thumping so hard that it hurts.

"Are you listening to me, Amani?" he yells, his voice sounds funny. Different. Southern. He takes his eyes off the road for a minute to look at me and I realise it isn't Ryan at all. It's my Dad.

I wake in a sweat. I feel like shit. My breath tastes gross. I open my eyes and the room is spinning. I force myself to sit up. My clothes are sprawled all over the floor and the bed. Where are my shoes? I groan when I remember that I threw up in them and tossed them in the bin outside. How am I going to explain that to Mum?

I find my phone on my dresser. I've got missed calls and texts from Leo and Ryan.

RYAN: *Where are you? Am in the kitchen. U want a drink?*

LEO: *You okay?*

LEO: *Ryan said he can't find you.*

Why? Why did I drink so much?

ME: *Sorry felt sick. Bad hangover talk later x*

I send it to both of them before pulling the duvet over my head and going back to sleep.

It's after four by the time I wake up. I drag myself out of bed and stretch before making my way to the shower. The difference a shower makes! I actually feel alive again.

I chuck on an oversized t-shirt and a pair of joggers and make my way downstairs in search of water. As I get to the bottom of the stairs there's a knock at the door. I can hear Grandad's music playing from his bedroom. Mum is still at work. I open the door and Leo grins at me holding two takeaway milkshakes from Fabio's.

"I thought this might help."

"Oreo?"

He nods and I dramatically grab it out of his hand.

"Can I come in?"

"Sure." I lead him into the living room and we sit on the sofa.

"How are you feeling? You were knocking them back yesterday."

"I'm shocked you noticed with all the girls hanging off your arm," I shoot back.

Leo blushes. "Yeah I took letting loose too far. We couldn't find you yesterday and got worried. Me, Sanaa and Ryan were looking for you."

"Sanaa?" I can't hide my surprise.

"It's not like you to wander off. But also, seeing you hanging with Ryan, you seem different. You don't seem like you. Sanaa said you were smoking last night?"

"It was just one puff, it's not a big deal."

"It is a big deal because it's not you. Did Ryan pressure you?"

"No!"

We fall into an awkward silence. I take a sip of my milkshake but my stomach churns.

"I'll have it later," I say, putting the milkshake on the table.

"Are you really not going to tell me why you just left?"

"You saw me leave with your tongue down Dani's throat? What a talent."

I instantly regret it and wish I can take back the words but they're buzzing in the air. Leo jumps to his feet.

"Amani, are you joking? You're hanging out with Ryan but it's not okay for me to be with a girl? I've been here for you since you moved here, whenever you've needed me, I've dropped things last minute and tried my best to be there for you. You keep shutting me out. You did the same to Sanaa and that's why she doesn't want to talk to you. Maybe our friendship isn't good enough for you. If that's how you—"

It feels like I'm under water. His words sound slurred and everything looks blurry. I grip at my chest and close my eyes. This cannot be happening right now.

"Marni, hey are you okay?" I can feel his arms holding me. "Shall I get your Grandad?"

I can't bring myself to speak as I take small, shallow breaths. I grab his sleeve and close my eyes.

1. . . 2. . . 3. . . 4.

My breathing slows.

5. . . 6. . . 7. . . 8 . . . 9.

I manage a deep breath.

10. . . 11. . . 12. . . 13.

I loosen my grip on Leo's arm.

14. . . 15. . . 16. . . 17.

I slowly open my eyes as Leo pulls a chair close and lowers me into it. I keep my focus on the floor and study the pattern of the red carpet. It's outdated but familiar and gives me something to focus on.

"Are you okay? Has this happened before?"

I nod.

"Have you spoken to anyone?" I think about telling him that I've spoken to Ryan but I don't think bringing up his name is a good idea.

"I'm fine. It doesn't happen often." I finally look up at him. "I'm fine, I promise."

I can tell he doesn't believe me.

"I'm just a bit stressed that's all. I don't mean to shut you or Sanaa out. Sometimes I find it hard to express myself and I miss us all hanging out." A tear falls down my cheek. "My dad coming back has really confused me. I want to move forward but this is the same man that flung my mum across the room like she was a ragdoll. I've been trying to block it all out and hanging out with Ryan is fun but sometimes I'm not having fun and I'm forcing myself to. At the party I was just alone. He went off with his friends and forgot all about me. Sometimes I feel so lonely and I don't want to burden my grandad because he's already worried about Mum."

"You can always talk to me, you know that, but have you thought about counselling?"

I shake my head.

Leo holds my hands. "Is there anything I can do to help make this better?"

"I don't know."

I know I should talk to a professional about how I'm feeling but what if they say I'm depressed like Mum? How would Grandad cope with that? It took me so long to feel settled in Manchester but now it feels like I'm going backwards and I can't remember the last time I was just happy.

After Leo leaves, I spend the day catching up on school work. I've not been on my A-game and need to get back on track. Just as I've finished and am thinking about what Grandad will make for dinner my phone rings. It's Dad. I didn't even tell them that their gift came. They probably think it's been lost in the post. I feel guilty, but I don't want Dad to ask me about the wedding so I ignore the call.

As soon as the phone stops ringing, I unlock my phone and delete the missed call. I don't know why I do it but it somehow makes me feel less guilty. It feels a bit like the call never happened but then my phone pings.

DAD: *Hey Marni, just checking that you're okay? I haven't heard from you in a while. When are you coming up to London? Love you x*

I read the message twice, then scoff. Funny how he's concerned about not hearing from me now yet spent over a year with absolutely no contact at all. He doesn't even mention the bridesmaid gift so maybe he was genuinely just checking up on me.

I sigh and call him back. He answers after just one ring.

"Hey, thanks for calling me back. I've been worried about you."

"Sorry, I've been really busy with college and stuff."

"Oh, okay, I wondered if you had received a parcel from us?"

"Yep."

"Right and you like it?"

"I guess."

There's a brief pause. I wait for him to snap at me for being rude but instead he says, "I'm sure the hair clip will look lovely on you. Did you have a look at the bridesmaid dress options? The wedding is getting close and we want to order the dresses as soon as possible. No pressure though."

I haven't looked at it. The box is tucked away in my wardrobe.

"Dad I've not decided if I'm even going to be there yet. I want to meet Zoe first and I need to talk to you."

"Oh, yes of course, that's fine, I understand. How about Zoe just buys you a bridesmaid dress just in case?"

It's her money she's wasting.

"I guess that would be fine. I'm a size eight. Actually, I'm thinking of coming to London in a couple of weeks?"

"Sounds good. Just send over dates."

"Will do."

We say goodbye and hang up the phone. I go to my wardrobe and carry out the box. I open it and pull out the hair clip. It really is pretty. I look over the bridesmaids dresses and they all look good but I can't see myself at the wedding let alone in them. I can't deny that Dad is trying though.

The old Dad would have shouted at me for having the balls to talk to him like that. Old Dad wouldn't even ask what I wanted to wear, the decision would have been made already. I wish I could talk to Mum about it but I don't want to upset her. She's been in bed for the past few days and I'm sure mentioning Dad won't get her out of there sooner. Times like this I wish I was still talking to Sanaa. She would know what to do.

OCTOBER

TWENTY-ONE

The bell rings for lunch and I bolt out of class, grabbing my backpack and shoving my notebook in it on the way out. I rush down the corridor taking care to avoid getting caught in the never-ending crowds of students. Today it's my turn to buy lunch for Leo.

The canteen is hot and muggy, and the windows are fogged up. It's been thundering and raining outside and looks like it's going to throw it down with rain again soon—typical Manchester. Everyone has huddled inside, their clothes damp from the first downpour.

As I make my way across the slippery floor, my Converse squeak with each step. I grab us cheesy chips and a Coke each before making a beeline for our table, hoping that no one has taken it.

I can't see Leo. Ever since the talk at my house, things have been good between us. It's weird though, because I haven't heard from Ryan since the party and that was over a week ago. I haven't seen him around college either. At first I thought maybe he was sick but according to his active social media he's alive and kicking. I guess his attention is elsewhere, which sucks.

As I get closer, I realise someone is sat at our table with their back to me. I would notice that head of hair anywhere—it's

Sanaa. My heart jumps. Is she waiting for me? I hope she's ready to forgive and forget and we can go back to normal.

Megan Porter slides into the seat next to her, then Alicia Brooks climbs in opposite and just like that, the table is full. What was I thinking? Of course she wasn't sitting there waiting for me.

And where is Leo? I don't want Sanaa to see me standing alone so I leave the canteen. I sit on the college steps hoping that the rain holds till I finish my food. Then someone sits beside me.

"Hey stranger," Ryan says. He puts his arm around me like he hasn't just ghosted me for a week. "I've missed you. This for me? I'm starving." He takes Leo's chips and Coke without waiting for me to respond.

"Err, help yourself."

My eyes wander around Ryan's face—his jawline, those lips, cheekbones. I feel a raindrop and another and another, and then the second downpour we've all been waiting for descends.

Ryan shuffles closer so I can hear him over the noise of the raging storm. The smell of cigarettes and aftershave is intoxicating.

"Did you know I got a new car?"

How would I have known that? And hey, thanks for checking on me after I walked out alone from a party. It's like the words are on the tip of my tongue but I swallow them. I don't want to fight. He's here now.

"My car's just there," he says, pointing at a VW Golf in the college car park. "Let's go in and get out of the rain."

He grabs my hand and before I know it we're running through the rain. He unlocks the door of his car and we're inside, drenched and shivering. My chips are soggy and look gross. We look at each other and burst out laughing. His shirt is transparent and I can see the outline of every muscle.

Ryan fiddles with the heater and a blast of warm air blows out from the dashboard. He flicks the radio on and the familiar voice of Brent Faiyaz comes through the speaker. We eat our soggy chips and drink our Cokes. We're both silent as we eat, listening to the music and the rain falling on the windscreen and it feels right, like a movie that I don't want to end. I want to feel like this every day.

"How long have you had the car for, then?"

"My dad bought it for me. I've got a provisional licence and I drive slow so I'll never get stopped." He winks at me. "Do you wanna get out of here?"

I look back at college. I don't feel like going to class, or bumping into Sanaa but I've never walked out of college before. Ryan grabs my hand and it's all the encouragement that I need.

"Let's go," I say and Ryan throws our rubbish out the window. He starts up the engine leaving Kemble College behind.

We head on the motorway out of Manchester. I have no idea where we're going and I don't care. I finally feel at ease. We slow down as we leave the motorway and drive through bendy, country roads. The houses on either side of the road are huge, like mansions. I can't help but stare and imagine myself living in one.

"Where are we?" I ask pressing my face to the window as the rain becomes a light drizzle.

"Nearly there."

We turn the corner and I instantly recognise it from the pictures on Instagram—we're at The Edge. My tummy does a little flip as the car pulls to a stop. I've never been here but this is the prime spot for students to come and have sex. Why would Ryan bring me here? We haven't even kissed!

He turns off the car before reaching to the back seat. "Here put this on." He hands me a dry hoody that smells like him.

We get out of the car and the smell of freshly wet ground hits me. My phone vibrates in my pocket.

LEO: *Where are u? I'm in the canteen.*

Ryan is changing his hoody so I send a quick text.

ME: *Hey I waited but couldn't see you. I'm with Ryan. Will explain later x*

"Come on." Ryan has a lit cigarette in his mouth and reaches out to hold my hand. This time he doesn't offer me his cigarette and I appreciate it.

He leads me up a little rocky hill. I walk slowly so I don't slip on the stones and rocks. When we get to the top I gasp. I can see the whole of Manchester from up here. Sanaa was right about the views, it really is beautiful.

There is something about being here with Ryan, the fresh air scented with rain and the sounds of cars in the distance that makes it feel like we're far away from our complicated lives. I wish I could stay here. With him.

I sit on the edge of a damp rock and Ryan sits beside me. His body is close enough for me to feel his warmth.

"Nice, right?"

"It's beautiful."

"So are you."

I press my lips together; I can feel it coming up from my stomach. I try to hold it in but I can't. I clasp my hand over my mouth to hold back a laugh.

"What's funny? I was trying to have a moment!"

I burst out laughing. "No, I know. I'm sorry. It's just I know why guys bring girls up here. It's a nervous laugh."

"It's cute. I like your nervous laugh."

We both look at each other. I notice the sun bouncing off his blue eyes. They look like they're shimmering in the light. I stare a little too long and he notices.

"Why are you hanging out with me?" I ask before I can stop myself.

"Why not? You're cool and fun—a little bit odd!" He smiles at me and the butterflies start whizzing around my stomach. "You look cute too, with these." He touches one of my braids.

I'm confused, a few weeks ago he was asking me to do something else with my hair.

His hand travels up my arm, to my neck where he pauses before he gently clasps my jaw in his hands and pulls my mouth to his. I lean in and allow him to lead the way as our lips meet. He parts my lips with his tongue, and pulls me closer to him. He tilts his head slightly, all the while keeping his lips firmly pressed to mine. He tastes of cigarettes and mints, but it's not as unpleasant as it sounds.

A few moments pass before he pulls away, I don't open my eyes straight away. I want to savour the moment. He kisses the top of my forehead before pulling me close to him and I inhale, breathing him in. This is surreal. I've just kissed Ryan Bailey! We stare out across the city. This is my favourite moment ever.

But he didn't even come after you when you left the party.

I shake my head. I don't want any negative thought ruining this.

"You alright?" Ryan raises his eyebrows at me.

I nod and close my eyes. Okay, he may not be perfect, but for now he's mine.

Ryan drives me back home and parks around the corner, just in case Mum or Grandad are home and waiting for me by the door. It's after four and I wonder where the time's gone.

"What time's your last lesson tomorrow?" Ryan asks.

"Three. Why? Did you want to hang?"

"I finish football practice around that time so I can drive you home after?"

"Yeah, I'd like that."

He reaches over and kisses me and I don't know how but it's even better than last time.

TWENTY-TWO

I'm in the toilets at college when I hear them.

"Well, I don't know if they're together, together but they're definitely smashing," says the first voice.

I freeze wondering who they're talking about.

"Are you sure? She seems like a prude. I can't see her sleeping with anyone. I don't even think she's slept with Leo Powell, and they're always together," another voice says.

Leo? Wait, who do they think is with him?

"Yeah, but that's because he's Sanaa's cousin and she's really protective over him. Apparently she's warned Amani not to go near Leo. That's what Alicia said."

I jolt my head back. Hang on, they're talking about me? I don't recognise the voices and the gap between the wall and the toilet door is too small to really see anything.

"So, she's with Ryan Bailey now? How did she even pull that off?" A new voice enters the conversation.

"Well, that's what I mean, she must be giving him what he needs in the bedroom, otherwise why would he bother, right?"

WHAT? Is that what people think? That Ryan would only be with me for sex? I want to confront them and tell them that Ryan actually likes me for me, but will I make it worse? If I'm defensive will they think it's because it's true?

I hear the girls laugh and the door opens. I've missed my chance. When I can't hear them anymore, I flush the toilet and come out. I fight the urge to burst into tears as I'm washing my hands and the door swings open.

"One sec, I. . . oh, Amani, oh I didn't know you were. . ."

"I know," I snap.

It's that girl Chloe who was at the party. Why is she even bothered about me and Ryan when she was with someone else? This girl doesn't even know me, none of these girls do but they're making me out to be something that I'm not.

"Sorry we said. . ." Chloe trails off as her face turned a bright shade of red.

"For your information, yes, me and Ryan are together and it's not about sex. Sorry to disappoint you."

I don't wait around to see her reaction. I storm out of the toilets and pass the other girls who stare at me open-mouthed. I head towards the car park and Ryan beeps at me. I find myself looking around hoping no one is watching but it's pretty empty. I used to think being 'seen' was a good thing but I hate that people are gossiping about me.

Ryan's tall, lean silhouette climbs out of the car and bounds towards me. I notice a few of his friends are inside the car smoking and I'm confused. Isn't Ryan taking me home? Ryan beckons me over. I try to calm down after what just happened.

"Well, look at you," he says looking at my legs as we get closer. And I can't help but think if those girls are right and Ryan is just trying to sleep with me? He bites his lip. "Slight change of plan, I can't drop you home tonight. I forgot we've got this thing." He points back at the car.

"Oh, what thing?"

"I have to just go and drop them off somewhere."

"Fine." I cross my arms over my chest. This day just seems to be getting worse.

He reaches down and places his hand under my chin to tilt my head gently up to him. "Forgive me?"

I nod.

"Oh there's a Halloween party this weekend, you up for it?"

"Am I going to be left alone again?"

"No I won't do that again." He kisses me and I feel lightheaded. I can hear his friends cheering from the car but I ignore them.

"But it's not Halloween for two weeks," I say.

"Yeah but it's half term next week, so we can stay as late as we want."

Before I can answer he reaches into his pocket and pulls out a wad of cash. He hands me £30. I wrinkle my forehead in confusion.

"Get yourself a little something to wear. Something sexy, yeah?" He winks at me.

"Ryan I can't take—"

"You can." He closes my fist around the money. "Boyfriends treat their girlfriends."

Wait, did he just say what I think he said?

"So you're my man?" I ask but it comes out more aggressive than I wanted it to.

Ryan's jaw tenses. "What? Is there someone else?"

"No, of course not," I say quickly, pocketing the money. "Only you—promise." But he's still looking at me funny like I'm lying or something, so I tiptoe and place my hand behind his head and slowly pull him towards me. He places his hand on my lower back, his lips parting mine. I try not to think about everyone watching. His friends lean out of the car window and howl into the empty car park. They turn up the music and honk the horn.

Ryan gently pulls away and my feet land back on the floor. I didn't realise he picked me up. We both laugh and he turns to give his friends the middle finger.

Chloe and the girls from the toilets walk by, trying and failing not to look. I keep my head high and eyeball them until they're out of the college gates.

"Wow, that kiss was something." Ryan's looking at me like I'm a whole meal with all the trimmings. "I'll call you later. Let's do something tomorrow night. Just me and you, yeah?"

"Sure."

He waves and goes into the car as I walk towards the main gates. A smile creeps across my face.

I fiddle my keys in the door and gently push it open. Grandad is out with some of his friends from his Blackjack club this afternoon and Mum is probably at work, so I have the house to myself.

As I pass the living room, I overhear a noise; it sounds like someone's crying. I push open the door and I catch my breath when I see Mum sprawled out on the floor. The TV is off and the curtains are drawn. She's in her work clothes and they are literally hanging off her. How have I not noticed how much more weight she's lost lately?

As she lays on the floor, I can see her spine poking through her top.

"Mum, what's wrong?"

I kneel on the floor, putting my arms around her. She's so tiny. I stroke her hair and get a sudden pang of guilt. I suddenly feel responsible. We're supposed to be looking after each other and lately I haven't been paying attention.

"I've lost my job, Marns," Mum says in a small voice.

"What? Why?"

But it's like she can't hear me. She's shaking her head and says, "I've failed again. That's all I'm good for. You're better off with your dad and Zoe."

"Don't ever say that! I'm yours and I love you. You'll get another job soon Mum, I promise."

I feel my body shaking, fizzing from the inside. Not the good fizzing that happens when I see a cute guy. The bad fizzing that makes me short of breath and I feel faint.

I look around the room, *green cushion, brown carpet, cream rug*. No, no, no this is all wrong. I look down at Mum and try to slow my breathing.

1. . . 2. . . 3. . . 4. . . 5. . . 6.

But it's happening again and I can't stop it. I can't catch my breath. I gently move Mum off my lap and place a cushion under her head.

"I'll be back in a minute. I'll make some tea."

I walk into the kitchen gripping my chest. I try to take a deep breath, but it's shallow and my lungs hurt. One tear falls down my face, and then another, before I know it I'm crying so hard that I can't control it. I try to breathe in again—still shallow. I grip my t-shirt and pull off my coat. I feel like I'm suffocating. This can't be happening right now; I need to be there for Mum.

Yellow tiles, yellow kitchen towel, yellow seat cover, yellow sponge. Calm down Amani.

I take a breath and it's deep and satisfying. I loosen the grip on my chest and take another breath. I feel calmer. I listen carefully and I can't hear Mum crying anymore. I inhale and exhale slowly.

I wipe my face with my top and put the kettle on. While I wait for it to boil I throw the empty cartons of Mum's Pot Noodle in the bin. I make us both a cup of tea with two sugars.

"Here you go, Mum." I put the tea on the coffee table. I glance at her, still on the floor, with her head slumped on her chest. "Mum?" I kneel down and gently shake her but she doesn't move. "Mum!"

I shake her harder and a pill bottle rolls out of her hand. I pick it up and shake it. It's empty.

"MUM! Wake up!"

I check her wrist. Her pulse is very weak.

I grab my phone from my back pocket and dial 999.

"I need an ambulance, please!" I say as soon as the operator picks up. "Hurry, it's my mum. She's swallowed some pills. Please help."

TWENTY-THREE

The journey to the hospital is a blur to remember. Everything happened so fast—the ambulance arrived and the paramedics came rushing in and took over. I'd managed to get Mum into the recovery position—lying on her side, her mouth downwards but with her chin away from her chest to help her breathe, and just kept talking to her, stroking her hand and her hair, trying to stay calm. I knew I had to hold it together for her. I did my best. But when they arrived, I started crying. I haven't been able to stop since. They tried to get more oxygen into her.

If Mum dies, I don't even know what I would do with myself.

Now, I'm sat here in this private family room in the hospital, waiting. I have nothing but my phone, which is about to die and I didn't even think to bring a charger. I have a plastic cup of water and an unopened Wagon Wheel that they offered me when I got here.

I've been over it a hundred times in my head. What if I had come straight home? I could have talked her out of it then. What if I hadn't gone to make her tea? Had she already taken the pills? How many did she take? What if I didn't have that stupid anxiety attack? No matter which way I play it out,

I know I could have stopped all of this from happening and that makes me feel like the worst daughter ever.

I torture myself until the door swings open and Grandad comes rushing in. I've never seen him move so quickly. He pounces across the room and throws his arms around me. He lets out a long, loud cry that is like a dagger to my heart. Moments pass and we do nothing but hold each other and pray.

"Yuh okay?" he whispers.

I nod before I burst into tears. My face is squished against his chest and I've made a wet patch on his shirt.

Please God let her be okay.

There's a quiet knock at the door and a young doctor pushes the door open. She has thick, Afro hair pulled back in two twists.

"She's stable," she says gently.

We both breathe a huge sigh of relief, the first real breath in what feels like hours. Grandad squeezes my hands tight.

"She's asleep now, but you're more than welcome to come and see her. You can stay in this room until the morning so you can see her when she wakes up." The doctor puts her hand on my shoulder. "I know it's scary, but the worst is over now. You should eat." She nods towards the Wagon Wheel, but I can't even think about trying to stomach that right now. "You know, your mum is so lucky to have such a smart, brave, loving daughter. You reacted quickly and saved her life." She turns to face Grandad and pats him on the back. "You should be proud."

Grandad gently grabs my chin. "I'm always proud of her," he says looking directly into my eyes.

He kisses me on the forehead. I snuggle into his chest again with no intention of moving.

The hospital lights are harsh and bright. Mum looks pale and her lips have a blue tinge. But she looks more peaceful than I've seen her in months. I watch her chest rise and fall in time to the beeps on the machine. She has tubes going into her hands, nose and mouth.

The doctor who escorted us to Mum's room lingers in the doorway, but she keeps her distance to give us some space.

"What do they do?" I point to the tubes.

"Don't worry about them," the doctor says. "They're just giving her extra oxygen and fluids."

I can't help but question how low she had to be feeling to even contemplate doing this in the first place, to leave me and Grandad. I just want to hug her and tell her that she's going to be okay and we're here for her, always.

Grandad takes a step towards her and holds her hand loosely. "We love yuh," his voice croaks. He puts his head down unable to speak anymore.

"We need you, Mum," I whisper.

He kisses her hand. "Give 'er a kiss, Amani."

I lean over and kiss her on the cheek, which is surprisingly warm and soft.

"You can come back first thing in the morning," says the doctor as she opens the door wide for us to leave. I had forgotten she was still there.

She leads us back to the private family room and gives us a pillow and small blanket each.

"You can pull the chairs together and rearrange the furniture to make yourselves comfortable if you need to. I don't mind helping but my shift is almost over."

"No, no, you've helped us enough today. Thank you," I respond, desperate for her to leave so I can gather my thoughts.

She looks to Grandad and he nods to reassure her.

"Good night, try to get some rest," she says with a sympathetic smile, before leaving the room and closing the door behind her.

But I don't sleep. I stay up and watch Grandad, afraid I'll wake up and I'll find him on the floor like Mum. My heart flips every time his breath catches in his sleep. I watch him closely until he inhales again.

It's been twenty-four hours since Mum was taken into hospital. When she woke up the doctor with the Afro said she had agreed to talk to a counsellor later on today and they will assess her and decide on the next steps.

"Can I see her?" I ask but the doctor shakes her head.

"She wants to be alone but it's no reflection on you," she adds quickly. "Your mum did a desperate thing and feels a little bit embarrassed. Just give her time."

I just want to see for myself that she's okay. I must have cried a million tears thinking about Mum. My eyes are puffy and swollen. I feel like I could cry again at any moment.

The doctors advise us to go home and they promise to call us once they have any updates. I'm exhausted but my brain can't seem to shut off. It's impossible for me to sleep.

Once we're home I go straight to my bedroom and Grandad

follows me. His eyes are puffy too. He looks around my room before settling on the bed, and I sit next to him.

We lay staring up at the ceiling for a moment. Grandad fumbles for my hand and squeezes it tight. It reminds me of a nature programme I watched where the otters were holding hands and floating on their backs while they slept so they didn't float away and lose each other. I squeeze back. I don't want him to float away.

"She gon' to be fine, yuh know." He pauses. "She strong, like her mum, like yuh. All my women are strong. Strong minds and souls. We 'ave to be strong fo' 'er."

He struggles to sit upright; I push his back gently to help him. He leans over and kisses me on the head and then leaves the room, closing the door behind him. I fight back the tears and ignore the lump in my throat.

I pick up my phone and see text messages from Ryan that I ignore. I'm not in the mood for questions on why we didn't meet up today. I scroll through my phonebook, the person I really want to talk to is Sanaa, but I don't know how I'll cope if she doesn't pick up the phone. I keep scrolling till I get to Leo. I dial, praying that he'll pick up.

"Hey, Marni, you okay? I didn't see you at college."

"Leo, hey." I fiddle with one of my braids.

"You alright?"

I take a deep breath. "It's my mum. She's in hospital. She tried to. . . well, she attempted to overdose."

"Oh shit! Is she okay? Do you want me to come over?"

"She's awake, but she won't see me. The doctor said she's probably embarrassed or something, and I should give her time, but she's fine though. They're keeping her in for the next few days." I rub my face. "I knew she was in a bad way but to want to kill herself. She was just going to leave me and Grandad. Is this my fault?"

"No! Why would you think that?"

"Because I haven't been checking up on her. I've been hanging out with—" I stop myself before I say Ryan even though Leo knows who.

"It's not your fault, Amani. Please believe me when I say that."

I want to believe him but I don't. I should have forced her out of her room and made her eat something. She should have been in counselling since she left Dad. I can't even imagine my life without Mum. I thought moving here would be better for all of us but the only one that seems happy is Dad—even though he's the one who broke us. How is that even fair?

"I'm here if you need to talk, anytime, okay?"

I nod even though he can't see me. "I'll call you later."

Once we hang up I go over to my wardrobe and take out the box with the expensive hair clip and the pictures of bridesmaids dresses and stuff them into my bag. I'm going to go to London tomorrow and give it back to them. If removing them from my life will help Mum then I'll do it. Dad had already sent me money to book a train for when I'm ready.

I text him that I'll be there tomorrow afternoon. I don't care if he has plans. He disrupted our lives again, so I'll disrupt his.

TWENTY-FOUR

As soon as I arrive at Euston train station the mugginess hits me. The air is much heavier here. The heat in the station is unbearable, even though it's freezing outside. The excessive amount of people travelling at this time in the morning is a lot for me to take in. I don't miss it. It feels weird being here.

I wander aimlessly away from the platform. The train was fine, but the closer I got to London the more anxious I felt. I had to focus on my breathing to prevent a panic attack and that wasn't easy as I couldn't stop thinking about Mum the whole time. Grandad is going to call the hospital to see if she is up for a visit and he promised not to tell her that I was going to London.

As I work my way along the platform, men in business suits bustle past, knocking my shoulder as they rush to jump on their trains. Women in skirt suits and trainers power walk along the platform. Nobody seems to be keeping clear of the yellow line, despite the reminders. People text as they walk, weaving in between people, not bothering to look up. It's like being back in college. I take off my big puffer coat as I jump on the packed tube. The only empty seat is next to a teenager in a pair of badly-fitted, black, leather trousers.

My phone buzzes. It's Leo asking for an update. I should be able to open up to Ryan seeing as he's now my boyfriend but being so vulnerable with him makes me feel uncomfortable. So much has happened since our kiss in the car park.

ME: *In London heading towards Camden to talk to Dad. Will keep you posted.*

LEO: *I hope it does well with ur dad xx*

Two kisses. I lock my phone and rest my head back on the seat. I pop my earphones in and I try to think of anything but Mum in that hospital bed. I try to imagine Zoe's face. I wonder if she looks like Mum?

Third stop: Leicester Square. Okay, I'm really nervous now. Soon I'll be at Camden Town, from there it's just a short walk to Dad's place. I'm glad he moved out of our old house; it would be weird going back there, especially after everything that happened. I don't know if I could step inside there again. That house has too many painful memories.

The train stops at Camden Town and I step on to the platform, searching for the exit.

I check the address again on my phone. This is definitely the place, but it wasn't what I was expecting. It's a brand-new, high-rise apartment block. I feel underdressed just standing in front of it. It's the complete opposite of the house that we lived in on the other side of London. This looks like something from an episode of *Black Mirror*, modern beyond belief, sleek, mostly glass and so tall I can't see the top of it from this side of the road.

I pull my earphones out and shove them into my pocket as I walk up the grey steps and the glass doors automatically open. When I cross the threshold I notice how plush the carpet is underfoot. There's a chandelier that hangs above an empty desk in the reception area. This looks more like a hotel than an apartment block. A few people fuss with their coats preparing themselves against the bitter cold. Their clothes look designer and their perfumes smell expensive. I feel out of place in my puffer jacket and take it off.

A middle-aged brunette lady, looks me up and down, clearly assuming I'm in the wrong place, before helping her husband to zip up his coat. I throw her my dirtiest look and make my way further to the reception area.

"Can I help you?" asks the concierge from behind her desk. "Are you here to meet someone?"

"Yes, my dad. Levi Brown. He's in number 45 but I can just call him to come down and meet me."

"It's fine sweetie, I've already buzzed," she says holding the phone receiver in her hand like a prop. "Hello? There's a young lady here to see—okay I will let her know." She hangs up the phone. "Ms Zoe Burton will be down in a minute. You can take a seat over there." She smiles and points to the round, cream sofas that are in the middle of the reception area. I make my way over and sit down.

Why isn't Dad coming to greet me? Why is it Zoe? My chest feels a little tighter. I try to focus on something else. This sofa is not as comfortable as it looks. I sit on the edge of it and try to slow my breathing. Cream sofa, cream carpet, cream. . . this is too easy here. Everything is cream and bland. I snort, a little amused by how boring this place actually is. My breathing slows down.

Two white families emerge from the stairwell to the right of the concierge, the children are polite and well spoken. They look cute in their uniforms. The parents are talking, the men are in suits and the women in running gear. Where the hell am I? As they pass, the children look me up and down and the women pretend not to notice me, but I see them exchange a bewildered glance when they think I'm not watching. I've never felt so Black. I have no clue how Dad and Zoe can live here.

The lift pings and out steps a woman. She's young, pretty, mixed raced, with her curly hair in a messy bun on top of her head. She has huge brown eyes and a petite nose. As she turns to face me, I catch a real look at her. She's gorgeous. She could be my mum a few years ago, before she lost all the weight and her skin gained its greyish hue. As she walks towards the concierge desk, her floral maxi dress sways around her ankles like a real-life princess.

She suddenly spots me and smiles. I politely smile back, the way that Black people do when they spot another Black person out of context. She has a brief conversation with the concierge and then, she changes direction and starts walking towards me.

"Amani?" she says as she gets close enough for me to hear.

"Hey." I stand up. "Are you Zoe?"

"Yes, it's nice to meet you," she says, holding out her arms for a hug but I don't move.

She drops her arms to her side and steps back, looking

around to see if anyone is watching but the reception area is quiet now.

"Your dad's popped out to get something for us to prepare for lunch, but he's caught in traffic. Sorry, he won't be long, but you can come up now if you want? It would be good to get to know each other." She tries to smile, but it comes off awkward.

I look her up and down. What does she have that Mum doesn't? This feels wrong. I can't go up there and play happy families while Mum is lying alone in a hospital bed. I've made a huge mistake. I should never have come here.

"I have to go," I mutter as I grab my bag and look for the exit.

"Please, Amani, come upstairs. Just 10 minutes and if you still want to go after that, you can go. Please."

I'm surprised that Zoe has tears welling in her eyes and I can see she's desperate to talk to me and then it hits me, maybe she's in trouble. I bet Dad is hurting her like he hurt us. An old shiver runs through my body. What kind of person would I be to leave her if she needs help? Mum found it hard to tell people what was going on and when she did it was dismissed. I don't want to be that person.

"Okay, 10 minutes," I eventually say.

"Thank you." She smiles at me and nods towards the lift. "After you."

TWENTY-FIVE

Their apartment is lovely. It's modern and decorated in cream with hints of vibrant African art on the walls and sculptures standing proudly in the corners of the rooms.

As soon as I walk in, I'm greeted by a strong smell of incense, which reminds me of our old house. Mum used to love burning that stuff. I don't know why she stopped. As Zoe leads me through the apartment, I spot some of our old furniture—a dresser in the hallway and a lamp on a desk, as we pass what must be a study. How can Dad be living this life of luxury with *our* furniture while Mum literally works herself to the bone?

"Would you like a drink? We have orange juice, water, lemonade, tea, coffee, or I can call your Dad to pick you up something?" She laughs nervously.

"Water is fine, thank you."

"Sit, sit, I'll get some snacks too." She fluffs one of the many cushions on the sofa as she leaves the room.

I perch on the end of the cream sofa so I don't dirty it with my jeans. I feel like I'm part of a spread in House and Home Magazine.

I spot a photo of Dad and Zoe on the side table and I stand up to inspect it. She looks elegant in a purple dress with her curls framing her face. Dad looks happy. They both do.

I wander back into the hallway, wanting to get a better look around. I push open the door to the office I saw on the way. I step inside the big space, feeling nervous as I was never really allowed in Dad's office at our old house. I slowly make my way over to his desk. It's littered with scraps from bridal magazines and handwritten invitations.

I pick up one of the invitations and it's addressed to my Aunty Nora, my dad's sister. She was the only person that Mum reached out to when she needed help. Does she ever wonder what happened to us? I've always been curious, what lies did Dad tell his family about why we left? We were completely abandoned by all of them when we moved to Manchester.

There's a pinboard above the desk filled with 'wedding inspired' colours and swatches. I touch some of the silk swatches and they feel as expensive as they look.

I leave the room and venture further down the hallway. I can still hear Zoe banging around in the kitchen. I push open another door and flick the light on. I step back and gasp.

What. The. Fuck?

It's a nursery, decorated with rainbow wallpaper on one of the walls. There's a half-built cot and a wardrobe in the corner. There are piles of children's clothes and teddies scattered all over the floor.

I look around confused. Do they have a baby? Where's the baby? Is Zoe pregnant?

I back out of the room, my heart racing. I grip my chest, but I don't count, I don't try to refocus, I just let the attack take over. I slide down the wall and crouch on the floor.

A baby.

I feel my forehead gather with beads of sweat and I can't even remember when I took my last breath. I'm such an idiot. I thought she was in danger and she's having his baby in this fancy house with a fucking concierge service.

I lean my head back on the wall and close my eyes. I automatically start to take small shallow breaths.

"Amani? Amani!"

I hear a tray hit the ground. The shattering of the plate and glasses bring back memories, I flinch at the sound. Zoe kneels down beside me and places her hand on my head.

"Shall I call someone? Do you need anything?" she asks.

I prise my eyes open and look at her and that's when I see it. As she kneels next to me protruding out from under her maxi dress is a tiny baby bump.

Zoe helps me up and leads me to the sofa in the living room. She goes to the kitchen and hands me a glass of water which I down in one go. She lays out a tray of expensive biscuits while I lay on the cream sofa not caring if I make it dirty. She asks me for the millionth time if I'm okay.

"Better, thanks."

"I didn't know which biscuits you like, so I put some of each out." She says nervously. She rubs her bump as though it's a magic lamp. It's very small, like Mum's before she had the miscarriage.

"Do you know what you're having?" I ask.

She looks away from me. "A girl."

A sister.

"When is she due?"

"A couple of months after the wedding."

And my dad didn't say a word. I wonder if Mum knew and if that's why she tried to hurt herself.

"Dad never said anything about a baby."

"I know and I'm really, really sorry about that. I thought that was why he went to Manchester. I'm so sorry that you're hearing about it from me but I would love to get to know you, if you'll let me. I want you to be part of my life and your sister's." She sounds sincere, but I can't bring myself to respond. "Was your mum okay with you travelling alone?"

How dare she speak about Mum? She has no right to talk about her.

I sit up and glare at her. "Did you know?"

Zoe hesitates. "Did I know what, Amani?"

"Did you know about me and Mum when you started having an affair with my dad?" The word *Dad* comes out through gritted teeth. My fingernails dig into the palms of my hands.

"I—I—" Zoe runs her fingers through her curls.

Look at her in this expensive house with a baby while my mum's in hospital. It's just not fair. I stand to leave.

"I'm sorry." I put on my jacket. "I have to—"

"Hello!" shouts Dad from the front door.

Zoe jumps up and waddles to the living room door. "We're in here, Levi."

Dad greets her with a kiss on the cheek and touches her bump. She steps back and they look into each other's eyes, but they don't say anything.

"Amani, how are you?" Dad makes his way into the living room but Zoe remains at the doorway.

"I'm going for a walk," Zoe says. She gives Dad a knowing look. "It was nice to finally meet you, Amani."

I don't even look at her. I hear the door close and now we're alone for the first time in over a year.

Dad takes his time putting his coat away. He sits on the chair opposite me.

"Look how beautiful you are." He smiles at me, but I don't return it. He awkwardly rubs the back of his neck. "I'm sorry I didn't tell you about the baby. I just wanted to see you and I thought it would be too much telling you about Zoe and the wedding and then the baby as well. I'm sorry that you found out like this. That's not the way I planned it."

"How did you plan it? Were you going to just bring a baby to Grandad's house and say 'surprise'?"

Dad flinches at my harsh tone. I see his fist clench and it all comes flooding back. I knew it! I knew he hadn't changed.

Dad takes a deep breath and unclenches his fist. "I'm very sorry. Can you forgive me?"

I jerk back in surprise. What is this new calm tone of his?

"Mum's in hospital," I blurt out.

"What?" Dad jumps to his feet. "What happened?"

"She tried to kill herself," I say in a matter-of-fact tone.

I watch him carefully as he paces the room, rubbing his jaw. A rage is bubbling up in my stomach. This is all his fault. He ruined our lives. I want him to feel just an ounce of the pain that we've been feeling. Dad's eyes well up and he quickly wipes them. That makes me even more pissed off. I don't remember him crying when he was beating her up.

"Grandad has been looking after me because Mum has given up and it's all your fault."

"Amani." Dad pauses. "I can see how you might think that the two are related, but your mum has been through a lot. The hospital might be the best place for her. You don't understand right now, but one day you will. I know you're scared and upset but she will get better."

He places his hand on mine and I pull it away disgusted. I can't believe he's trying to pretend that he has nothing to do with this!

"What I can understand is that you cheated on her, caused her to lose her baby, physically and mentally abused her, and if that wasn't enough, you also had to come round to *our* home, after a year of nothing, to tell her that you're marrying the woman you cheated on her with. So you're right, she has been through a lot. But *I'm* right when I say that it's your fault."

Dad's face hardens, his body tenses up and for a second I really think he's going to hit me but then he closes his eyes and exhales and his face softens. It happens so quickly that I almost think I imagined it.

"I'm so sorry about your mum."

"What exactly are you sorry for? Sorry for hitting her? Do you hit Zoe too?"

"Amani stop!" He clasps his hands together as if he's praying. "I want us to move forward. I want you to be part of our lives. I'm going to be a dad and I want you to help me to get it right this time."

It's like a knife to my heart that has been twisted round and round.

"You're already a dad!" I roar. "I'm not done needing you and you left me. I'm still your child. It's like you've forgotten that." I pick up my bag. "I should go."

"I didn't mean that. This is hard for all of us. Amani, can

you just wait a second?" He reaches out for my arm and I snatch it away.

Our eyes meet and there it is. The rage bubbling inside him, it hasn't gone completely. He can pretend all he wants, but I can see through it. He hasn't changed.

I turn to leave and he grabs my arm. His fingers dig into my skin, but I do what I wish I did years ago. I push him off and he looks at me surprised.

I pull my arm free and instead of going to the front door, I walk to the study.

I take out the hair clip from my bag and throw it so it bounces off the wall. I hope it's broken. I rip up the print-out of the bridesmaid dress and the pieces flutter to the floor like confetti. I swipe my hand across the desk knocking over the stack of invitations.

As I leave the study Zoe is coming through the front door but I push past her and run straight out the corridor.

"Amani!" she jumps back and shouts after me. I don't stop running until I get to the lift. I press the button, frantically willing it to come quickly.

"Amani!" Dad shouts after me. I can hear his heavy footsteps. Memories flood back of what life was like with Dad. I hear him shout again, "Get back here right now!"

The lift comes and I jump in pressing the buttons quickly.

The doors close on Dad's face.

TWENTY-SIX

I don't know how long I've been here. I've lost track of time. It's getting dark and the hustle and bustle of London's nightlife is beginning to emerge. The suits and power blazers have been replaced with skinny jeans, glam crop tops and heels.

"Do you want anything else?" the waitress asks, instantly snapping me out of my daze.

I've been sitting here staring out of the window for God knows how long. There's an empty cup in front of me that I don't remember ordering. I wiggle my tongue around in my mouth to try to remember the taste and remind myself what I've drunk. Tea? Hot chocolate? I don't know. I shake my head at the waitress and she takes my cup and walks away.

My phone vibrates. I've lost count of the number of times Dad has tried to call since I left his apartment. I look at my screen. *Give up, I don't want to talk to you.* I turn it down on the table.

My attention returns to a clumsy group across the street. A man and woman have broken away from the rest and they're at the end of the road just out of sight of their friends. Their hands move rapidly over each other's bodies like snakes in a basket. The man cups the woman's face in his hands and pulls her to him and they kiss. It's like a movie kiss that goes on forever. His hands run up her skirt, up to her thigh, her bum, they stop, they squeeze, caress, her hips dance into his and I turn away. I've seen enough.

I push my chair away from the table and stand up to leave. The cafe is empty apart from an old lady on the other side who has several bags. She seems too engrossed in the conversation she's having with herself to notice me, but the waitress sees me looking at her and offers me an amused smile.

I don't smile back, I'm not amused. I leave the café and the air hits me like a truck. I have to take a moment to steady myself.

I don't remember walking to the train station or getting on the train but before I know it, I'm already halfway back to Manchester. I check my phone; my battery is dying and I have so many missed calls from my dad, one from Grandad, Ryan and a text from Leo. I call Grandad.

"Hello," he answers the phone straight away.

"Hi, Grandad, it's me."

"Yuh okay? 'im call me, I been trying t'call yuh! I'm glad yuh safe."

"I'm fine, I'm on my way home now. Did you see Mum?"

"No, not today but she soun' good on the phone."

I sigh in relief. "I'll see you soon. Love you."

"Love you too."

I hang up the phone. I don't want to go home yet. I just want to erase this shit day. I close my eyes to try and clear my head, but I can't.

Zoe couldn't even say that she wasn't having an affair with Dad. Does she even know who she's making a family with? I wish I'd told her everything.

I want something to take my mind off all of this. I drum my fingers on my lap and then I remember the Halloween party. That must be why Ryan called me.

ME: *Hey are you still going to that 'Halloween party tonight?*

RYAN: *That depends, you wearing something hot?*

I look down at my jeans and trainers. My makeup is a mess too but I want to get drunk tonight.

ME: *Of course, I'll be there*

RYAN: *Meet you at there? I'll send the address*

ME: *Cool, on the way X*

I look at my phone to check the address one last time before paying the taxi driver with some of Ryan's money. He'll be pissed that I didn't use it for an outfit but I don't care.

The street is littered with Kemble College students who are drinking from various bottles and plastic cups. Most are dressed in poor attempts at Halloween costumes; I pull my jacket around me to help hide the fact that I haven't dressed up.

I text Ryan to let him know I'm here. While I wait for him to come and meet me, I eyeball a couple on the steps. The guy, who I don't recognise, has his arm around a small, red-haired girl's shoulder. She looks like most of the girls at Kemble. She's smiling and babbling away telling him some story, and her eyes are drooping a little as she speaks. I think it's from the alcohol. He doesn't seem to mind though. As he watches her, he looks as though he is falling more and more in love with her, he's hanging on to her every word. She's confident and beautiful. The confidence is probably the alcohol talking and she's almost shouting with excitement as she speaks now. I need some of that confidence.

I feel a tap on my shoulder.

"Hey you." Ryan throws his arm around me. He squeezes me close and my head fits just comfortably under his shoulder. "Let me see." He pulls away and opens my jacket. "Where's your outfit? Is it in your bag?"

To distract him I grab the cup from his hand and down it in one go. The after-taste burns my throat.

"Hey you," I say in a husky voice. "Why are you so sexy?"

A smile creeps across Ryan's face and I can see he has totally forgotten about my outfit. "Let's get you another drink."

He leads me to a crowded hallway and I'm immediately hit with the loud bass from the music. People are shouting to be heard over the music. We weave through the couples and groups until we reach the kitchen.

Ryan reaches into the bucket and pulls out ice. He places it into two cups.

"Vodka or rum?" He's pouring vodka into his own cup.

"Either."

I couldn't care less what I'm drinking as long as it helps me to forget today. Ryan hands me a cup and I take a sip. It's stronger and less fruity than whatever he was drinking. I wince at the taste and Ryan laughs.

He takes a sip of his and recoils. "Fuck, that's strong."

We laugh and tap our cups together.

"Cheers," we say in unison.

I take another sip and this time it doesn't taste so bad.

"Let's go somewhere quieter," he whispers in my ear.

Taking my hand, I follow him through the patio doors into a small, paved garden. Pretty fairy lights lace the fence on either side. Cigarette smoke fills the air and swirls around the tiny patio. The music sounds muffled out here and it's the right volume for us to be able to have a private conversation.

I take a deep breath and look around, and for the first time today I feel at ease. I relax my shoulders and let my bag fall to the floor. I suddenly realise I've turned up to the party with my big college backpack.

My stomach rumbles. I haven't eaten since this morning. I take another sip, and another. I feel slightly lightheaded, but it feels damn good, like I'm floating away from all my problems. Ryan smiles, his eyes reflecting the fairy lights. This is exactly what I need.

A girl turns around. She dressed as Catwoman with her full black leather. I can only see her eyes. I smile at the effort. I think the alcohol is kicking in. My eyes follower her as she leaves the garden and goes into the house.

I reach up and stroke Ryan's arm and his face lights up.

"Come here." He pulls me towards him while fumbling with his phone. He holds it up and takes a picture of us together. I look awful, he looks incredible, of course.

"Yuck, delete it," I say scrunching up my nose. I try to step away to face him, but I stumble. He grabs my arm to steady me.

"Careful." He laughs and starts typing on his phone.

"I'm fine!" I throw my head back and chug my drink. I smile and hand him my empty cup. "See!"

"I'm impressed." And he looks it. "I'll be one minute—wait here."

He walks into the house, oblivious to the girls whose eyes follow him as he walks. They're so jealous that he's here with me. A few girls look me up and down but I don't care. DaBaby plays through the speakers. I love this song! For the first since Mum went into hospital, I feel free. *I feel happy.*

My phone starts to ring and it's Leo.

"Hello," I sing down the phone.

"Marni, are you serious? You've come back from London and gone straight to the Halloween party? You could've called me to let me know you were back safe. Don't do anything stupid, okay?"

"Where are you?" I turn too quickly trying to find him and stumble again. I burst out laughing.

"Ah man are you drunk? Are you with anyone?"

"I'm with—" I look around but I'm by myself. Where did Ryan go?

"Here you go." Ryan appears, handing me a glass. "Who you talking to?"

"Leo," I say and Ryan takes the phone off me.

"Leo my man! Why you always ringing my girl? You want me to hook you up with someone? Nah, she's busy. Peace." Ryan hangs up the phone and taps my shot glass. "Drink up."

"Is Leo okay?" I slur.

"Don't worry about him."

I throw the shot back and instantly regret it as the alcohol burns my throat. I let out a squeal.

"Well done!" He bites his lip. "Why don't we go upstairs and hang out?"

He smiles and that dimple makes my heart flutter. I feel like the only girl at the party. I feel seen.

"Okay," I say throwing the cup to the floor.

As we make our way through the house, he grabs a bottle of vodka from the kitchen and hands it to me. I spot the girl in the Catwoman outfit from the garden and she's staring at me again.

Ryan has both hands on my shoulders and he's shouting above the music to one of his friends as we walk by them. I feel dizzy. I grab Ryan's hand pulling him quickly through the crowd to the stairs. I just want to get away from everyone.

He takes the bottle of vodka from me and has a swig before grimacing and handing it back. I hold it firmly and take a swig for myself, as we unsteadily climb the stairs.

We reach a white, wooden door. Ryan pushes it open and turns on the light. There's makeup scattered across the desk, clothes hung in front of the wardrobe and a bed, a large double bed. My eyes flick to it. Ryan is staring too. I take another swig of vodka, this time longer than before.

Come on confidence juice, work your magic.

TWENTY-SEVEN

This bed is really uncomfortable but I don't care. I feel like I'm floating on a cloud. London feels like it happened months ago. Ryan's busy rummaging in his pockets looking for something. He smiles, looking satisfied, before coming to sit beside me. I suddenly realise that he hasn't bothered to dress in a Halloween costume and that makes me laugh so much that I'm doubled over.

"What's so funny?" Ryan asks. But I can't even remember, it just feels good to laugh.

Ryan reaches over and cups my face in his hand and I immediately stop laughing. My head is spinning and my heart feels like it's beating out of my chest. I lean towards him as he pulls me close and presses his lips against mine, tasting of alcohol. As we kiss harder and faster, he pushes me back on to the bed so my head is on the pillow. His hand starts to move up my body and he fumbles to find his way under my t-shirt. His fingers find my bra and I wince and pull away, feeling uncomfortable.

I'm not ready.

"Ryan—"

"It's okay" he whispers, pressing his lips to mine again. His hands move towards my jeans.

No! This doesn't feel right.

I clumsily try to push him off me. I want to shout 'Stop' but for some reason the words don't come out. My jeans are by my ankles and I feel so cold. Ryan moves his mouth away from mine for a second and pulls a condom out of his shirt pocket. Then his fingers move over my knickers.

I think I'm going to throw up. I use all of my force to push him off me and it sends him rolling off the bed, landing with a loud thud.

"What the fuck, Amani? What's wrong with you?" He pushes himself up off the floor, red-faced.

I swallow down the bile that's rising in my throat. My blurred vision starts to clear as I fumble to zip up my jeans. I flick the condom that's on the bed at him and it hits him on the chest.

"What's wrong with *me*?" I growl, pointing at myself.

"What did you think we were coming upstairs for? You knew this was going to happen. Don't play stupid."

I step away from him but lose my balance and have to steady myself on the dressing table. "I'm not ready for sex."

He stands up and wraps himself around me and I feel claustrophobic. "Are you scared it will hurt? I'll be gentle I promise. Come on let's just do it. You don't know the effect you have on me."

He pushes his hips forward so I can feel him. I can feel the bile racing up my throat again. I push him away and hurry to the door just as it swings open. Catwoman is standing in the doorway.

I rush past her and out of the room with my hand over my mouth and I make it to the toilet, just in time, as I throw up into the sink. I wipe my mouth with the back of my hand and catch myself in the mirror, not even recognising the sad girl looking back at me. I wipe a string of vomit from my mouth. What am I even doing here? Suddenly the bathroom feels too small, the music is hurting my ears. I need to get out of here.

I throw open the bathroom door and rush out in the hallway. Keeping my head down I run down the stairs and out of the front door. Everything looks fuzzy. I can taste alcohol on my tongue and I regret every sip. I can smell Ryan's aftershave and I wipe my mouth wanting to erase his kisses.

The cool air hits me and my stomach rumbles. Oh no. I run to the corner of the garden and I throw up over red roses. I cripple over and fold to the floor as my stomach cramps and forces me to heave. I feel like it will never stop, like my insides are trying to escape.

I try to steady myself but my body feels like a dead weight. I stumble to the side and fall over next to my own vomit.

My phone vibrates, and at first it takes me a moment to react. I try to sit up and reach into my pocket. Leo's name flashes across the screen. Leo! I need him. I need him to help me. I swipe right to answer it and will myself to speak but I can't. I look down at the phone but I can't hear anything that he's saying. I feel dizzy. Maybe if I lie down for a second, everything will just stop.

When I open my eyes, I'm in a bed, wrapped up under a quilt. It smells familiar but it's not home. I force my eyes open and the room is dark apart from a tiny slit of light coming from the door. I climb out of the bed and drink the water on the desk next to me.

My head is heavy and my arms and legs feel like they belong to someone else. I'm bare foot and I notice my trainers are in the corner. I open the door and the room instantly fills with light. I immediately recognise the hallway and it clicks into place. I'm at Leo's, but how did I get here? Where is Leo? Does my Grandad know I'm here? *Shit!*

I slowly walk down the hallway, to the room at the end where I can hear the sound of the TV. I walk into the living room and Leo and his parents are sitting together on the sofa. I watch them for a moment before they notice me.

I've always been jealous of Leo's family. His parents are so in love, they're like a poster for how to maintain a happy marriage.

"Hi," I say sheepishly.

His dad notices me first and nudges his mum. "Here she is."

She stands up and hugs me. "Are you feeling any better? Can I get you some more water?"

I nod. "Yes please."

Leo's mum holds my shoulders and looks at me at arm's length. She tilts her head and then pulls me in for another hug. I'm suddenly conscious of how bad I must smell, after all the travelling, drinking and throwing up. I pull myself away, but I smile to show I appreciate the hug.

"You gave us quite the fright, but we're just happy you're okay. I'm going to fix you some toast as well." She leaves and her husband follows her into the kitchen.

I can't help but stare. The relationship Mr and Mrs Powell have is so unfamiliar to me. I envy Leo for growing up with them and being surrounded by so much love.

Leo's looking at me like I'm a stranger.

Say something, please say something, I plead with my eyes.

The sound of the TV fills the silence.

His eyes move across my face. "This isn't like you." He stands in front of me and holds my hand. "Let me in, Marns."

Mr Powell walks back into the room and Leo drops my hand. His dad places two drinks and some toast on the table.

"There you go. We're just in the other room if you need us."

"Thanks," I say gratefully as I watch him leave.

"What happened in London?" Leo asks gently.

"I saw my dad and Zoe. She's pregnant."

"For real?" He raises his eyebrows in disbelief and he sighs.

"But it's fine, it's fine," I say.

I don't even know what I'm saying, I mean it's not fine but I don't want to talk about it anymore, especially with this hangover. I turn to face the TV and notice a teleshopping channel is on. There's a woman in a ginger wig trying to sell an awful seashell bracelet. Teleshopping usually comes on after midnight

"What time is it?" I ask. I take a seat beside him.

"1:30am."

I groan. "Grandad's going to be so pissed with me. I've got to go home."

How could I be so selfish? Grandad already has enough on his plate

"It's fine," says Leo. "My mum already spoke to him."

"Does he know I got drunk?"

Leo shakes his head. Thank God.

"You were in such a state. I found you laying down next to your own sick. You couldn't have gone home."

I look away, embarrassed. If I felt shit before I feel worse now.

"What did Ryan do to you Amani? It's just when you answered your phone you said—"

"Let's not do this." I shake my head and keep my eyes fixed on the television.

"You're doing it again," Leo snaps and I look at him surprised. "You're shutting me out."

He's right. I need to stop pushing away those who actually care about me.

"I'm sorry. I was so upset about Dad I didn't want to go home. I wanted to get drunk and forget about everything." I close my eyes. This is hard enough to say without seeing Leo's face. "Ryan wanted to have sex and I didn't. He wasn't taking no for an answer. I wasn't ready despite the rumours you may have heard."

"WHAT?" Leo yells and I jump. He stands to his feet and I've never seen him this angry before. His nostrils are flared and his fists are clenched. I'm sure if Ryan was here he would be knocked out. "Did he try and force you?"

"I pushed him off but I don't know, maybe I was giving him mixed signals. I was so drunk."

"Having too much to drink is not a reason to make a girl feel uncomfortable and force her to have sex. Don't make excuses for him ever, you hear me?"

Leo's right I need to stop making excuses for his behaviour. And then it hits me. For all my judging to Mum about not leaving Dad sooner, for trying to justify him, I managed to do exactly the same as her. That ends now. No more excuses.

"I hear you." I slide my hand into Leo's and squeeze it. It instantly makes him calm down and he sits down beside me.

"Ryan's always been a dick, even when we were kids. He treats girls like their disposable and that's why I didn't want you with him. He's a user and you don't deserve to be treated like that. You're special, Amani."

"Special." That word feels strange on my tongue. It's everything that I'm not, and clearly Ryan thought that too. A hot tear strolls down my face, another then another.

"Please don't cry." Leo gently wipes my face with his thumb. He's still holding my hand. I take in his hazel eyes, his floppy curls, his tight jawline. He is so beautiful. I lean towards him and my body tremors. The pit of my stomach flutters with butterflies and my head feels full of air.

"Amani." He breathes my name and I want him more than anything. "I want this."

"Me too."

"But not like this, not after tonight. I'm so sorry, but you deserve better."

Instantly, the bad thoughts telling me I'm not good enough creep into my head but this time I quickly dismiss them. I don't want to keep entertaining them. I hold on to the fact that Leo likes me back. I lean into him feeling his heartbeat through his chest and without a word he holds me tight. I smile to myself realising he must like me loads to ignore how bad I smell! We watch the television until eventually we fall asleep wrapped up in each other's arms.

TWENTY-EIGHT

Even though it's the half term break, Leo has football practice at college pretty early, so his mum drops me home first thing in the morning. The streets are busy and the car journey with this hangover is making my head spin. I can't stop thinking about last night—the alcohol, the party, Ryan. Thinking of him makes my stomach churn. My head begins to ache as I cringe at the memories.

I hold my head in my hands as we pull into my street and I try to focus on the good parts of last night—laying on the sofa with Leo, him telling me that he wants me and the way it felt to have his arms wrapped around me. I can't help but smile.

We pull up outside my house and his mum cuts the engine.

"Thanks again for everything," I say. "I'm so sorry about coming round so late last night. It won't happen again."

Mrs Powell squeezes my hand. "Don't apologise love, it was really good to see you. It has been months since you came round. We miss seeing you, Leo, and Sanaa together."

"Yeah me too," I reply sadly.

"You know, I shouldn't really say this, but you're very special to Leo. Let's just say he thinks highly of you. We all do. I know you've been having a hard time but we're all here for you."

I squeeze her hand back. "Thank you."

I wave her off and watch as her car turns the corner before I go to the front door.

"You're home!" Grandad throws his arms around me.

I hug him back and breathe in his scent, so familiar and comforting.

"Marni." He pulls away and looks directly into my eyes.

My heart instantly sinks. "Is it Mum?"

"Yes, but she's okay. She alright." A tear leaks into the soft creases next to his eyes "She ready to see yuh."

"She is? When?"

"We'll go first thing tomorrow."

I just finished changing after a long shower when the doorbell rings. Grandad has popped to the shop to get some groceries so he must have forgotten his keys. I open the door slowly and I can't believe it. Sanaa's here.

She reveals a small box she had been hiding behind her back and holds it out to me. "I'm so sorry about your mum."

I fight back tears as I throw my arms around her and drag her inside. "I've missed you so much."

"I've missed you! I got this for you and it's not even gifted."

I open the box and inside is a beautiful gold necklace with my name on it.

"Now we match," she says, holding her own identical necklace out for me to see.

"This is lovely. Thank you."

"I know it doesn't make anything better. How are you?"

I sigh. "I don't even know where to start. We haven't spoken in so long. Did Leo tell you about my mum?"

Sanaa nods. "I couldn't believe it. I picked up the phone so many times but I just thought that you wouldn't want to hear from me. Then I saw you at the party—"

"You were at the party?"

Sanaa hesitates. "We don't need to talk about that now. I just wanted to check in and see how you were doing and I'm just so sorry for what I've said, and ignoring you and just being a shit friend."

I grab her hand. "I've been shit and I'm sorry. Can we be friends again?"

"Of course! I love you girl and I'm here for you, always."

"Always," I echo.

My mind races as we walk down the corridor to Mum's room carrying a bouquet of colourful tulips—her favourite. She's sat up in bed resting against three big pillows. She still has that distant look in her face that she's had for months but her cheeks are flushed with colour. Her eyes widen when she sees us in the doorway. She gasps and holds her arms out to us.

I drop the flowers on the table by the door and Grandad and I rush towards her.

"I've missed you both." She squeezes us in a hug.

"We've missed you too," I say.

"I'm so, so, sorry. I should have never put either of you through this."

Grandad pulls away first. "Yuh dun need t' hexplain yo'self. We need t' look t' da future now." Grandad gently strokes Mums cheek.

Mum turns to me. "Amani can you give me and Granddad a minute?"

"Sure, I'll just be outside."

I find a vending machine a couple of corridors away and I rummage in my purse for some coins. I pay for my tea and sit on one of the cheap grey seats in the corridor. I pull out my phone and send a text to Leo.

ME: *Sanaa came by today and we made up. I'm at the hospital and Mum is doing well. Thank you for last night.*

I hover on the send button before I add.

ME: *Sleeping in your arms was the best sleep I've had in years xxx*

He texts me back straight away with the love heart eyes emojis and I swear I melt.

I finish my tea and make my way back to Mum's room. As I enter, Grandad stands and kisses me on the forehead before leaving. Now me and Mum are alone. Mum pats a space on her bed and I sit beside her.

"Are you feeling better?" I ask.

Mum smiles. "Yeah baby, a little. I have a way to go but I'll get there. I want to say thank you. I wasn't thinking straight. You saved me." Mum pulls my hand to her lips and kisses it. "My hero."

"You're my hero," I say to Mum. "Hey, no more tears."

I wipe them away and Mum laughs.

A doctor knocks gently and pushes the door open without waiting for a response. He's really tall and skinny with thin blonde hair and glasses. Grandad follows behind him.

"Hello, I'm Dr Burden, you must be Amani?"

I nod.

"I've have been caring for Ms Matthews while she's been here. As you can see, she's feeling much better. She has no lasting physical damage and she is fit and healthy. However." He pauses and flicks through his notes. "We would like to keep Ms Matthews in for a couple of days to support and monitor her. She has agreed to continue to see our counsellor while she's here and together with our Mental Health Liaison we will assess the next steps. We want your mum to be at home with you as soon as possible but we just want to make sure that you and your Grandad have help to support her first. Does that make sense?"

He's looking at me waiting for a response.

Yes, it makes sense but it's not what I want to hear. I want to take her home now.

"Is that what you want, Mum?" I ask.

"I think it's for the best," Mum says. "I want to get better and I want to feel happy again."

"We'll support you with whatever you need," I say and Grandad nods in agreement.

"Brilliant, I'm glad you both understand and I'm happy that we're all on the same page," Dr Burden says. He closes his notes. "Amani, can I have a quick chat outside?"

I hop off the bed and follow him out of the room.

"Am I right in thinking that you're the one who found your mother after her overdose?" I nod. "You did such an amazing job and you responded so quickly. You should be very proud of yourself."

It's weird because I don't even think I did anything special.

I did what any child would do for their parent but I can't believe how close I was to losing her. I pray Mum gets all the help that she needs so we never have to go through this again.

"But how are you doing?" Dr Burden asks. "How have you been since that day? Have you been sleeping okay? Would you like to speak to anyone about what happened? Sometimes having a counsellor can help you to process how you're feeling. Would you like me to set up an appointment?"

The idea of reliving this moment over and over again with a stranger isn't something I can handle right now.

"For the moment I don't think it's for me but if I change my mind can I get back in touch?"

"Of course. We're here for you. It's going to be a long road and this is just the beginning but we're heading in the right direction."

"Thank you Doctor, for everything."

He smiles at me which makes his eyes crinkle up. "That's what we're here for. I'll leave you to spend time with your mother."

I wave goodbye feeling relieved that Mum is going to be okay. We both are and it's been a long time coming but this time we're going to be okay. I just know it.

NOVEMBER

TWENTY-NINE

I'm wrapped up in my warmest coat, scarf and gloves but I can still feel a chill. It's getting so cold now, it's what Grandad would call 'hibernation weather.' I wish I was still in my bed but Leo wanted to meet up and I couldn't say no. I assumed Sanaa would join us but it's just me and Leo, which is basically a date, although he never actually said so.

"I swear you're exaggerating." Leo's looking at me and laughing. "What are you gonna do when it gets colder and starts snowing? Wear your quilt? I've never met anyone so dramatic."

"Leave me alone! I can actually still feel the cold air under all these layers trying to freeze me to death."

He rolls his eyes at me. He's only in a light jacket. I don't know what point he's trying to prove.

We're on the way to the fireworks display at the park. I love fireworks. The colours, the music, the way I always try to catch a picture of one going off and it never does it justice. A girl from college is having a party tonight and everyone's going except me. That Halloween party is still fresh in my memory, and frankly, I can't see myself partying until at least fresher's week at university next September.

As we enter the park Leo stops to talk to some friends. I recognise them but I don't know any of their names. He introduces me and we say hello. I look around and it's pretty packed. The food and drinks stalls are scattered around the park and I spy a cheesy chips stand.

Someone tall and muscular is walking toward me. I would know that walk from anywhere. It feels like ages ago that I would obsess about Ryan, but seeing him now, all I feel is anger. I haven't spoken to him since the Halloween party but I feel ready. Plus, I feel safe with so many people around and Leo beside me. I take a step forward but I don't think Ryan sees me because he walks by like I'm not even there.

"Ryan," I say, a little louder than I meant to, and he stops walking. He turns to me and I can't read his expression.

Leo automatically stops his conversation with his friend. I hold my hand up to let him know that I'm okay. Leo turns slightly and angles himself to keep an eye on us as he continues talking to his friends. I'm grateful for the protection.

"Oh. Hey," Ryan says sharply "How are you?"

What is with the attitude? I'm confused what he has to be mad about.

Ryan crosses his arms and glares at me. "I actually wanted to speak to you, somewhere private but, you know what, here will do. I know that party thing got a bit weird but we were *both* drinking." I open my mouth to object, but he speaks first. "Coach called me today. He got an anonymous call that I have a drinking problem. I don't have a drinking problem."

"I never said—"

"You know, I would have more respect for you if you came to my face and told me how you felt, but to tell Coach that I attacked you is out of order. I've been suspended from the team until they investigate. Are you happy now?"

"Huh?" What is he talking about? "I thought. . . are you not going to apologise?"

Ryan's eyes bulge like I've said something crazy. "You've ruined my life! Football was my one chance to be something. I don't have a back-up plan. I didn't attack you, so why is there a witness saying they saw us? Yes, maybe I read the signs wrong but you were coming on strong, Amani. I thought you wanted to take us to the next level. That's what girlfriends do."

"Just because I'm flirting doesn't mean I'm down for sex. No means no, Ryan. And for the record we are not a couple!"

He doesn't respond.

I have no idea what witness he's talking about. It was just the two of us in the room but there's a niggling feeling in the back of my head. When I left the room, someone was at the door. . . who was it?

Leo walks over and stands beside me. Ryan throws his hands in the air and laughs, but the sound chills my blood.

"Of course, you were in on it as well. Always sticking your nose in."

"I don't know what you're on about but you need to calm down," Leo says and Ryan squares up to him so they're nose to nose.

"Or what?" Ryan hisses and I see Leo make a fist.

I pull Leo back and stand between them. I take a long look at Ryan and I can't believe I even liked him. How is *he* the victim? This is what Dad would do to Mum, do something terrible but somehow turn it on her.

"I never told your Coach anything but I wish I had. You're such an entitled dick. You come over here and you can't even apologise!" I'm shouting now and people are looking over but I don't care. "You don't even call me to see if I'm okay. I actually liked you, like really liked you. I was out here smoking, drinking, skipping class, even changing my hair for you. And then you try and sleep with me when I'm drunk? I'm glad you got dropped, you deserve nothing less."

I push past him, too upset to keep talking. I feel Leo grab my hand as we walk away and I'm grateful for the support.

"Who was the witness?" Leo asks as we get to the other side of the park.

For a second I thought maybe it was him.

"I don't know but someone was at the door when I left. I just can't remember who."

"I should have knocked him out."

"He's not worth it." And he really isn't.

The crowd seems to thicken, if that's even possible, but luckily we have a good spot. Leo moves behind me and wraps his arms around my waist so his hands are clasped in front of me. I rest my hands on his. How are his hands so warm? He nuzzles his face into my neck and I squeal as it tickles.

There's a howling whistle as the first firework goes up in the air. The crowd fall silent, then there's an almighty bang as flecks of colour litter the night sky. Another goes up and the crowd cheers and claps. There's something about the way the colours light up the night sky that makes it feel so magical. I take a picture of them on my phone and laugh when, as usual, the picture doesn't capture how bright the colours are. The crowd naturally hustle and bustle around as they watch the display. I can feel the heat from Leo's breath on the back of my head. I feel safe in his arms. I could stay wrapped in them forever. I don't even need to look at him to know that he's smiling too.

As we leave the park, we hold hands and make our way towards my house. We walk really slow, trying to make the journey last as long as possible.

"Leo," I say at the same time he says, "Amani."

We laugh.

"Go on," he says nodding at me.

"There's just something that's been on my mind. It's just now that me and Sanaa are back on speaking terms, where do me and you stand? I mean, ever since that night I stayed at yours, we've gotten closer and I like it a lot. I want us to be more than friends but if we decide to have a relationship then we need to tell Sanaa upfront. No more secrets."

Leo rubs the back of his neck. He steps closer towards me so I can see the green and brown in his eyes. "I want us to be more than friends too."

Every fibre in my body wants him to kiss me. My heart starts to race. My lips pucker up showing my impatience that I want him now. His lips are soft and full and fit perfectly with mine. In my mind I can hear the fireworks still howling and exploding around us. It feels like they're spinning and fizzing in my tummy.

At first his kisses are gentle but then they become harder and more urgent. I follow his lead but then our tongues meet and he groans and lifts me up.

"Leo!" I laugh and he swings me round.

"What are you doing to me, girl?"

He puts me down and this time he leaves little kisses from my neck to my jaw before kissing me again on my lips. I don't want this night to end.

THIRTY

Sanaa waits for me outside my Sociology class. She's leaning against the wall using her phone as a mirror, as she applies her lip gloss, oblivious to the people looking at her as they pass. She's dressed like Cher in *Clueless* with her short tartan skirt, tights, heeled boots and a turtle-neck jumper.

Her eyes light up when she sees me. We link arms and make our way down the corridor, dodging the crowds. A few people glance at me apologetically. They clearly heard about me and Ryan. I see Chloe walking out of the girls' toilets with some of her friends. She gives me a timid wave and I ignore her.

I glance at Sanaa who's oblivious. Things don't feel exactly as they were before we fell out but I don't think that's a bad thing. I'm different. I'm way more grown and I feel like I know who I am but more importantly the type of person I want to be.

I'm trying to open up more too. My problems feel easier to deal with now I'm not bottling them up. I can talk about Mum without feeling like I need to keep her condition a secret and it feels really good.

Sanaa and I have spoken about Tyler and how she really feels about him. She can see the red flags in some of his behaviour but she still wants to give him a chance. I feel like I would have been so judgemental before, but I'm realising that Sanaa is a smart girl and needs to make her own mistakes. I'm going to be there for her no matter what happens.

We weave through the canteen until we reach our lunch table. We sit down just as Leo arrives with some sandwiches and chips.

"Perfect timing! I'm starving." Sanaa reaches across the table, grabbing a handful of chips from his tray.

He flashes me a smile while Sanaa shoves more chips into her mouth. That smiles makes me feel hot all over. I take a deep breath remembering that Sanaa's here and we haven't spoken to her yet.

"So, Marni, you must be so excited to see your Mum later?" Sanaa grins. "I'm so happy that she's agreed to come home this weekend."

When the doctor called Grandad this morning saying they were discharging Mum it felt like all my birthdays had come at once. The house hasn't been the same without her.

"I can't wait to just chill out with her. Grandad's going to cook her favourite meal and we're all gonna relax and enjoy having her home."

"And what's happened with your dad? Has he been in touch?" Leo asks.

I shake my head. I'm not surprised to not have heard from Dad and honestly I don't miss him. There's not even been one phone call to see how I am or to check on Mum. It's clear to me that he's still the same selfish person he always was and we're better off without him.

"I'm just getting a drink." Sanaa stands up. "You lot want anything?"

"A Coke please," Leo says.

"Me too," I echo.

As soon as Sanaa walks off, Leo sits closer towards me, his leg pressed against mine.

"Hey," he says softly.

"Hey." I smile.

His hand finds mine under the table and our fingers entwine.

"When are we going to tell her?" I ask. "I don't want to keep us a secret."

"Soon, I promise."

Mum's asleep on the sofa, wrapped in a soft blanket. When she arrived home a few hours ago I started to panic, what if she wasn't ready to be back home? Although she looked tired, she also looked happier than I've seen her in a long time. I thought she would be hesitant in coming into the living room because this is where she overdosed, but thankfully she was fine.

I'm sitting opposite her watching her sleep. Grandad is cooking in the kitchen and the smell is filling up the house. My stomach rumbles and just as I think about going to grab a sneaky piece of whatever he's cooking, Mum's eyelids flutter and settle on me.

"Baby girl." Mum slowly sits up and I hurry over to help her. I sit beside her and she leans into me. "How are you feeling?"

"So much better. I feel light in a way I haven't felt in a long time. I'm sorry again Marni for putting you in that position. I should never have done that."

"It's okay, I'm just glad you're better." I hesitate. "I saw a leaflet in your bag about depression a while ago. Did you go to a support group?"

Mum shakes her head. "I wanted to but just the idea of going and saying it all out loud was terrifying. It would make it so real. I even booked an appointment for the doctors but then I cancelled it. The longer I left it the more I kept falling down this black hole and it was like I couldn't see a way out, but baby, it had nothing to do with you or Grandad okay?"

"What about Dad?"

Mum brushes imaginary dust from the blanket over her legs. "Seeing your dad didn't help and hearing about his wedding and baby—"

"You knew?"

Mum nods. "But he said he was going to tell you himself. Grandad said you went to London to see them. I guess it didn't go well?"

"Not all." I sigh. "I haven't spoken to him since."

"Since you visited him, he's been calling your Grandad every day to check in on you. Grandad told him to give you space but he did call to speak to me at the hospital."

"Really?"

"He's not perfect by far but I can see that he's trying in a way he's never managed before. Let him try, baby."

I thought Dad didn't care about us. Not only did he try but he respected Grandad's wishes to give me space rather than forcing his presence on me. I suddenly feel like I'm bursting and I want to tell Mum about Ryan and the party and Leo. Especially Leo, but I don't want to overwhelm her.

"Grandad's in the kitchen whipping something up," I say standing up.

"Oh, I don't have much of an appetite."

She waves her hands in front of her face and I see how slim her wrists are. Now, looking at her properly, I see her face is gaunt and her neck is thin. She looks at my face and she must see the worry and panic as I eyeball her.

"Actually I will have a little something," she agrees and I'm grateful as I didn't want to have to beg.

We walk to the kitchen and Grandad has filled the table with dumplings, ackee and saltfish, callaloo and plantain— all of Mum's favourites. The smells fill my soul. I look at Mum and I smile because I know she feels the exact same way.

We sit at the table just as Grandad brings over some sliced hardo bread.

"Dinner fit for two queens." He beams.

"Aren't you eating Dad?" Mum asks as I notice the table is only set for two.

"Nah, nah, I ate a likkle summin while I was cookin.'" He rubs his tummy. "Yuh two need to talk and eat." He kisses Mum on her hair.

Mum holds his arm. "Thank you, Dad."

"Thank you, Grandad," I echo.

He leaves the kitchen and Mum and I look at the food and then at each other.

"This looks so good!" she says helping herself to some ackee and saltfish.

"Better than Pot Noodle?"

Mum laughs. "Oh so much better."

We eat in silence but I can feel Mum watching me.

"What do you want to do about Dad's wedding?"

The question takes me by surprise. I dish out more food to allow myself a minute to think.

"I don't know," I say truthfully. "I think I need to talk to him again properly."

"You know my counsellor, Karen, told me that a big part of my recovery depends on me being transparent with my thoughts. Talk to your dad but also listen to what he has to say, it's the only way you both can heal and move forward."

I feel conflicted. On one hand thinking of Dad leaves a sour taste in my mouth but hearing the effort that he's put in makes me question if shutting him out is really fair. I was horrible to Sanaa and to Leo, but they gave me a second chance regardless of what happened.

If Grandad told him to leave me alone then that means I need to make the first move and I'm not sure if I'm ready for that. I don't want him to disappoint me again. But at some point we have to move forward and if Mum is making an effort to do that then maybe I should too.

After we eat, Mum goes back to sleep on the sofa. Grandad sits with her so I go to my room. I take a deep breath and call Dad.

"Amani," he answers breathlessly on the first ring as if he ran to the phone.

"Hey, Dad."

"Oh I'm so glad you called. I've been wanting to talk to you since you came to London. I'm actually in Manchester—"

"You're here?" I switch my phone to my other ear like it will help me hear better. "Why?"

"Your Grandad told me your Mum was getting discharged this week. I actually wrote her a letter, well—I wrote one for both of you, but I realised this was something I wanted to do in person. I want you both to hear my apology. Your Grandad was going to update me if I could see your mum. I obviously don't want to make her more upset. Can I see you, though?"

"Oh." I grip the phone. "I don't know."

"Please, darling. I'm staying in town but I can drive down and will be there in 10 minutes. Just please hear me out. Please."

I don't think I've ever heard Dad sound so sincere before. I can almost hear my defences coming down.

"Okay," I say quietly.

"Thank you. I'll see you in a bit."

I'm waiting outside my house wrapped in my coat. Mum and Grandad are still asleep. I'm trying to give Dad the benefit of the doubt but I'm staying close to the doorstep so if anything goes wrong, I can scream for help and Grandad will rescue me.

An Uber stops in front of my house and Dad steps out. He thanks the driver before walking towards me. I hope I'm not making a mistake giving him another chance.

"Hi, Amani," Dad says, standing a few steps away from me and giving me space, which I appreciate. "Thank you for meeting with me. How is your mum doing?"

"She's okay, she's asleep. Before you say your piece do you mind if I go first?"

"Oh no, of course," Dad says.

"I don't know how I feel about you. I want to move forward but I need some clarity. Why did we have to live in fear of you? Do you know every morning I would wake up wondering if today would be the day that you killed my mum? And I don't understand why you made us live like that. We didn't deserve that life!"

"I know," Dad says quietly, looking at the floor.

"How is it fair that *you* get to live this life of luxury and Mum is working multiple jobs to hold us above water? You're getting married with a new baby, yet Mum ends up in hospital. How does that even make sense?"

Dad looks up and I can see his eyes are welling up. "Amani, I'm so unbelievably sorry for everything that happened. I don't even deserve a second chance. I don't deserve your forgiveness, but I'm begging you for it. The way I behaved, the way I treated your mum and my complete lack of compassion was not okay and I'm sorry. I've been in anger management and counselling for almost a year and I've learnt a lot about myself." He wipes his face. "I've had so many issues from my own upbringing and I'm a work in progress. I will always keep trying to do the right thing. Zoe knows about my past and has stuck by me while I'm working to get better. I love you so much, Amani and I will spend the rest of my life making it up to you."

Dad's shoulders are shaking and it takes me a moment to realise he is crying. I walk over to him and wrap my arms around his waist. He sinks into me like a little boy.

"I'm sorry, I'm so sorry," he says over and over again.

Now I'm tearing up. I can't even remember the last time I hugged my dad. I've been so scared of him that being in arms reach just was never an option. I'm glad that he's recognised that he needs help and is getting it. I wish he had got it sooner and maybe, just maybe, our family could have been saved. But maybe Dad needed to lose us first to see what that he was the problem.

"I have something for your Mum." Dad pulls away and hands me a small, white envelope. "Can you give this to her?"

I nod and hold on to it.

"I've written down everything that I've wanted to say since you both left. If she ever wants to see me, I would love to apologise to her in person—when she's ready."

"That would be good." I play with the envelope in my hand. "Did Zoe know you were married to Mum when you got together?"

Dad hesitates before he nods and there it is, the truth. I thought I would feel angry but I just feel numb.

"She was under the impression that our marriage was over and I was leaving. That was all on me though. I didn't show any respect to either of them. I've never hit Zoe but I've definitely lost my cool. She pushed me to get help and I wanted to. I'm not proud of the man I was but I'm starting to like the man I'm turning into. I wish I could have been a better man for you and your mum."

My dad is a complex man. Sometimes he's cruel, scary, harsh but he's also funny, spontaneous and now I can add genuine. . . because I believe him. I believe that he's trying and wants to be a better person. This version of my dad I can deal with. I want to get to know this man who wants to do right by people.

"Thank you for being honest," I say. "I'm glad Zoe is a positive influence and you're getting help because now we can work on us."

"I would love that so much," Dad says. "More than anything in the world."

He reaches into his bag and hands me the gold hair clip that I threw in his house. I'm surprised it didn't break. He also gives me a wedding invitation. It's cream and what feels like expensive paper.

"I hope you can at least attend?" Dad asks.

December 8th. My dad is really getting married. God, I hope he doesn't mess this one up. I look up at him and smile and his eyes light up.

"I'm sure I can do more than that."

When I go back into the house, I'm not surprised to see that Mum and Grandad are awake.

"How was it?" Mum asks.

I hold up the invite. "I guess I better get ready to be a bridesmaid."

"I think that is a good choice," Mum says.

"Proud of you." Grandad winks at me.

I hand Mum the envelope. She looks at it then back at me with her eyes wide. "From him?"

I nod. "I think it's worth reading."

THIRTY-ONE

There's a knock at the front door and the postman stands on the step, shivering in his shorts in the bitter cold, holding a parcel.

"Amani Brown?" he asks as soon as I open the door.

"That's me."

He asks me to sign for the parcel before he hands it to me.

"Thanks," I say but he's already walking off. I close the door and make my way into the living room with the parcel in my hand. I sit down and tear off the brown parchment paper.

"Who's that from?" asks Mum, she's curled up on the sofa in her dressing gown.

She's been eating more regularly and her face is looking fuller. She looks good. After reading the letter from Dad, she called him and they spoke on the phone for hours. It's like the conversation took it out of her because she fell into a deep sleep but in the morning she looked brighter, like a weight had been lifted off her.

It's a cream box. I take the lid off and there it is. I gently pull the forest-green silk out of the box. It's beautiful, soft and elegant. It's the colour of a Christmas tree, dark and regal. I hold it against my arm and marvel at how it makes my skin pop. It feels smooth on my arms. I lay the dress on the floor.

Inside the box, hidden underneath the dress, is a pair of gold strap heels that match the hair clip.

I pull the shoes out and slide my foot in. It's a perfect fit.

"Wow, that looks gorgeous," Mum says. "Zoe has good taste."

"Yeah, she does."

Mum stands to her feet. "Come on then, let's try them on."

"Okay, okay," I say rolling my eyes but deep down I actually can't wait to put it on. I've never worn anything that feels so expensive.

We get to my room and Mum sits on my bed. I slip my tracksuit off and slide the dress and shoes on. I gasp when I see myself in the mirror.

"Oh my God Marni, you look so beautiful." Mum's eyes well up.

I look really good. The dress hugs my curves and the colour is perfect for my skin tone. My feet look dainty in the gold heels. I look like a grown up and I like it.

"Wait let's see it all together."

I walk slowly to my wardrobe—it's going to take me a minute to get used to the heels—and pull out the first parcel.

"What's that?" Mum asks and I forgot she hasn't seen it yet.

"They sent me this when they asked me to be a bridesmaid." I don't mention that it was actually returned back to me. I hold the hair piece and it really is stunning. I hand it to Mum and she gently traces her fingers along it.

I wonder what she's thinking. This is the first time I've really thought about the heartache she must have felt watching someone fall out of love with her. Trying everything to make it right and still ending up as their punching bag.

This is the first time I've thought about not just the physical damage he's caused her but all of it, the whole thing is heart-breaking.

"This is really beautiful," Mum says. "When me and your dad got married it was really simple with just family and a few friends. He mentions our wedding in the letter he wrote me. Said it was still one of his favourite days of his life." She stands ups and comes behind me. "It's one of mine too, but I'm happy that he gets to start over."

"You will too," I say even though I can't imagine Mum with another man.

Mum grabs a hair scrunchie from my dresser and bundles up my braids. She slides the hair piece in and it completes the whole outfit.

"Perfect," Mum whispers. "Me and your dad did something right."

After I've sent a text to Dad to tell him how great the dress looks, I get changed and start on some school work. Mum heads downstairs but it's not even five minutes later when Grandad knocks on the door and peeps his head around the door without waiting for me to respond. I swear you get no privacy with Jamaican grandparents.

"Want to help me cook? I'm making chicken and rice."

"Sure, I'll do the rice."

I follow him down the stairs and into the kitchen where everything is already set up: bowls, spoons, rice, herbs, spices, peas soaking.

I begin to pour some rice into a pan to rinse, while Grandad rolls up his sleeves, ready to wash the chicken. At first, we move around the kitchen without speaking, just dancing and swaying our hips and humming along to Taurus Riley. Grandad sings sweetly as I hum along to the melody.

After he washes the chicken and makes a paste from the herbs and spices, he coats it and puts it in a tray in the fridge to marinate. He washes his hands and sits at our little kitchen table. I finish up seasoning the rice and peas and place a scotch bonnet in the pot before turning on the cooker. I sit with him at the table.

"Marni, you're okay, aren't yuh?" Grandad asks cautiously.

I haven't seen him this nervous since that night in the hospital with Mum.

"Yeah I'm okay," I say truthfully.

"Good." He keeps his eyes fixed on the table. "Yuh, mum's gonna be fine."

I don't know if he's asking me or telling me, but I say, "The three of us are going to get through anything that life throws at us."

"Yuh n yuh mum, you're my rocks, you know dat?" I see his eyes well up and he keeps his focus on the table, not wanting to make eye contact. "I need yuh, bot' of yuh. I need bot' of yuh to be fine." His voice quivers and I don't know what to do. My grandad is the strongest person that I know, it's strange seeing him like this.

I walk to the back of his chair and throw my arms around his shoulders. I bend down and kiss him on his grey, wavy hair. He smells of *Old Spice* and it's so comforting. I squeeze him tight and breathe him in.

"We're gonna be just fine," I say and I mean every word.

The rice is bubbling and the pan lid is struggling to stay calm over the boiling water. I can't help but feel that's what we've all been doing for so long—struggling to keep our lids on, while we're boiling up inside.

Mum comes into the kitchen. "Can I get some?" she holds her arms out.

"Of course." Grandad smiles as we make our way over to her.

She smiles back. A real smile that's beautiful and perfect.

THIRTY-TWO

"So, I was thinking."

Sanaa and I are sitting in the stands watching Leo play football. He almost fell to the floor when I agreed to come.

"What's up?" she asks.

I've already filled her and Leo in on my dad and the wedding, but there's one favour I still need to ask of Sanaa.

"Dad said I can invite a plus one to the wedding and I wanted to know. . . will you come with me?"

I'm not expecting her reaction. Sanaa squeals and claps her hands. "Girl, course I will! I'll be right by your side the whole time. This is all I've wanted from you, Amani."

"To come to a wedding?"

"No silly, to be let in! You're my best friend and I just want to be here for you, no matter what. Boo!" She jumps to her feet and points at the opposite team. "Foul!"

"Yeah, foul!" I echo, also standing up. I have no idea what's going on. All I know is watching Leo run in shorts is one of the best things I've ever seen.

I wish I had watched him play football sooner. He's brilliant and I have no doubt one day he will be a massive football star.

We sit back down.

"Did you mean it when you said that no matter what?" I ask.

"Yeah sure."

I take a deep breath. "Okay, well there's something I need to talk you about."

"Wait, can I go first?"

"Oh, okay." She seems uncomfortable and is shuffling in her seat. Why does she look nervous?

"Are you pregnant?" I blurt out.

Sanaa's mouth drops. "No!" She swats my arm. "It's about Ryan."

"Oh, what about him?"

"Okay so, I'm just going to say it."

Now I'm nervous.

"The night of Jessica's party, well, I followed you and Ryan. I just wanted to check if you were okay because you had been drinking loads, but as I got to the door, you ran out. I called you but you didn't turn around. I thought you didn't want to talk to me still, so I called Leo to come and get you."

She lets out a deep breath, as though she's relieved to finally get it all off her chest.

"I spoke to Ryan when you left to ask what happened but I mean I kind of guessed when I saw the unopened condom on the floor. He tried to say that you wanted it and he had been the one to say no!"

"Are you serious?" This guy really was something else. "I don't remember seeing you, though." All I remember seeing is—Catwoman! That was you?" Sanaa nods. "You came to help me? But you hated me."

"I never hated you, Amani." Sanaa sighs. "I was annoyed and upset. Of course I was looking out for you. I've known Ryan since we were small and he's always been an idiot. I knew you liked him and I can see why but I never encouraged you to go for it because of how he is. When I realised you were together I kept an eye on you both. I didn't believe those stupid rumours about you sleeping together for a second."

"Thank you. It means a lot that you said that."

"I told him that he better stay away from you and never even think of looking in your direction again or your dad would kill him."

I try not to laugh but it bursts out. "My dad?"

"I didn't tell him about your dad but you know, the thought of an angry Black dad protecting his daughter will scare any guy, right? I'm sorry for not telling you sooner."

"Even when we've not spoken in months you're still looking out for me." I throw my arms around her. "Thank you."

"Can we promise to never ever fall out again?" She holds out her pinkie finger.

"Not ever." I link my finger with hers.

"Good, because I also told Coach that he had a drinking problem."

"You told him?" I gasp.

"Damn straight." Sanaa flicks her hair. "I hope he learns his lesson. Look, Leo has the ball!"

We both turn back to the pitch as cheers erupt from the stands. Leo scored! My heart skips a beat as he looks up and blows me a kiss. *Shit!* Sanaa looks slowly at me and I look anywhere but at her. I can feel Sanaa's eyes burning a hole into the side of my head but I refuse to look at her. No way!

She nudges me. "Amani, look at me." I reluctantly turn to her. "I already know."

"What? How?"

Sanaa laughs. "Why do you think I wasn't being the third wheel on Bonfire Night? Leo was being over protective when you were with Ryan. No guy acts like that if he's not into you."

Is she saying what I think she's saying?

"So, you're fine with it?" I ask slowly.

Sanaa shrugs. "The train is already in motion. Just, if you guys break up, don't make it weird for me."

I scoff. "We're not official."

"Yet," Sanaa sings and I can't help but grin.

The idea of Leo being my boyfriend makes me feel good all over.

"I was only protecting you when I told you to back off. Leo's never been serious about a girl. He's usually talking to a few but he never seems interested in other girls whenever you're around and you seem more like yourself when you're with him. It's a good fit. Besides, after the few months you've had, you deserve some good."

"Thank you, Sanaa. You know I always thought you didn't think I was good enough for him."

"Amani, are you mad? You're too good for most of the boys at Kemble, of course you're good enough for Leo! Probably the only girl that is."

I don't think she has any idea how much it means to get her blessing.

I turn to watch Leo. He's dodging in and out of the other team and dribbling the ball to the net. He passes the ball to a teammate, only for him to immediately pass it straight back. Leo kicks the ball and it hits the back of the net. He scores again! We immediately jump up and down, applauding him. His eyes dart to me and he waves so I wave back. I love that when he scores he immediately looks for me.

Sanaa laughs and makes a love heart with her hands. I swat them away but I can't help but laugh too.

After the match we wait for Leo outside the changing rooms. He comes out with wet hair after his shower. I fight the urge to run my fingers through his curls.

"Well, damn, you were on fire today!" Sanaa says. "Can I get an autograph?"

"Shut up!" Leo says but he's smiling. "Well, was it worth coming?" He searches my face.

"Hmmm, it was okay." I tease.

Leo clutches his chest like I've just broken his heart. "This one is hard to please."

"Hey Leo, come over here, there's someone I want you to meet." His coach waves him over. He's stood beside a man in a big, blue and white coat.

"One sec." Leo runs over to them.

"Who is that?" I ask and Sanaa shrugs.

Leo does lots of head nodding and it seems like the man beside Coach is doing all the talking. After a moment they shake hands and Leo jogs back to us with the biggest smile I've ever seen.

"That's a scout from Leeds. He wants me to come and try out for his team next week. This might be it!"

"Oh. My. God. Leo, this is huge! Congratulations!" Sanaa hugs him tight.

"All I needed was my good luck charm." He flashes me that smile that just does something to me.

Oh sod it! As soon as he lets go of Sanaa, I tiptoe to gently press my lips against his.

"Oh my eyes! Get a room please!" Sanaa yells.

Leo bursts out laughing but he doesn't let go of me.

DECEMBER

THIRTY-THREE

I'm at the train station waiting for Sanaa in my green dress. Mum loaned me a smart black coat to go over it. I have my heels in my bag and vans on my feet. It's past eight and Sanaa's still not here. Our train is going to be leaving for London in a five minutes. She's not even texted or answered any of my calls. I try calling again and it rings.

What if something's happened to her? Sanaa is usually glued to her phone.

My phone vibrates and her name flashes across the screen. Thank God!

SANAA: *Can't make it. Sorry Marns but have fun!*

I read the message again and again. Is this a joke? Surely she's joking.

My throat dries up and I can't swallow. Why would she do this? I thought we were friends again. My eyes instantly well up and my nose starts to sting as I hold back the tears. I try to call her but she ends the call. My heart starts to race and my body clams up.

People rush by in the opposite direction towards the train. There's four minutes until it leaves. I try again and again, willing her to pick up. Why won't she pick up? I deserve some sort of answer, some kind of reason why.

Someone taps my shoulder and I turn around.

"Hope you don't mind that I'm here instead?"

Leo! I look him up and down and, wow, he looks good in a suit. He fills it out perfectly.

"You're coming with me?"

"If we get to London on time." He laces his fingers around mine and pulls me to the train. We board with three minutes to spare.

"I'm so confused. What are you doing here?" I'm struggling to take all of him in.

His suit is a sharp grey and he's wearing a freshly-ironed, crisp, white shirt. I usually only see him in sportswear. He is wearing a green tie that is the exact same colour of my dress. He's had his hair cut short; his loose curls are now neatly tapered into a neat high top.

"I wanted to be here for you. I'm your date and I promise to not kiss you in front of your dad even though you look incredible."

The way he's looking at me I believe him. He reaches across the table to hold my hand. I rest my hand in his and my whole-body tingles. It's like electric currents pulse through my body.

"Did Sanaa ask you to come?"

"No, I asked if I could step in, and she agreed."

"You asked?" I'm impressed. How lucky am I to be dating this gorgeous, mature, thoughtful guy?

"She actually gave me a lecture."

I groan. "What did she say?"

"Only that she was mad at me for not being honest with

how I felt about you and why I've not asked you to be my girlfriend yet?"

I catch my breath. He gets up from his seat across the table and slides in beside me.

"So, what would you say if I asked you to be my girlfriend?"

Is it normal that my heart feels like it's going to bounce out of my chest and across the table? I want to scream yes!

"I have to think about it," I tease.

"Maybe this will help you decide?" He leans in close to kiss me and I swear if I could be attached to Leo's lips all the time I would do it. He looks at me through his long lashes. "Have you made a decision?"

"Yes, I want to be yours." I whisper and this time when we kiss it feels different because this is the first kiss when he's officially mine.

After a tube ride and a short taxi journey we finally arrive at the venue.

"Ready?" he asks me.

"Ready."

Together, we make our way up the steps and there's a sign at the entrance that reads 'The Wedding of Mr Levi and Mrs Zoe Brown - Second Floor.'

As we enter the building, we're both taken aback by the beauty of it: tall ceilings, white pillars, sparkly chandeliers. This place looks like something out of a magazine.

A woman looking almost identical to Zoe walks towards us. She's wearing an outfit like mine. She has the same smile and same curls as Zoe.

"You must be Amani? I'm Bria, Zoe's sister, it's so nice to finally meet you! How was your journey?" She shakes both of our hands.

"Good, thanks, this is my. . . boyfriend, Leo."

"Nice to meet you," Leo says politely.

"Thank you for coming. The bride and groom are upstairs. I can take you up if you want?"

"Sure."

We follow Bria over to the lift and up to the fourth floor. She leads us down an expensive-looking long corridor with numbered doors.

"They stayed in the same room last night, even though it breaks tradition. Zoe was having pains and she didn't want to be without Levi," Bria explains, although nobody asked.

We stop at door number 419.

"Levi, Zoe, it's Amani and Leo," Bria calls as she knocks on the door.

My dad opens it a few seconds later. He's in a shirt and his suit trousers.

"Marni!" He pulls me in for a hug. "Wow you look beautiful."

"Thanks Dad. You clean up well. This is Leo."

Dad raises is eyebrows at me.

"My boyfriend," I finish.

I don't know what I expect Dad to do but I definitely don't expect him to shake hands with Leo so enthusiastically.

"Thank you for coming, Leo," Dad says.

Zoe appears in the distance behind my dad and waves. She's in a floral night gown and is cradling her bump, which seems to have grown a lot since we last met.

"Come in, come in," Dad says stepping back into their room.

"See you soon." Bria waves as she skips off down the corridor.

This must be the honeymoon suite because it's huge! It's at least three times the size of my room at Grandad's. The ceilings are high and the four-poster bed, decorated in draped silks, looks luxurious and opulent.

"You look beautiful, Amani," Zoe says as she struggles to lower herself on to the sofa with the weight of her bump. "Green is your colour."

"Thank you. I love it. How's the baby doing?"

Zoe looks at my dad and she can't hide her surprise. Dad smiles and nods at her.

"Your sister wouldn't let me sleep a wink last night. I'm exhausted." She sighs.

"Well, you look great," Leo says and Zoe eyes him up.

"Are you Amani's—"

"Boyfriend," Dad adds. I can't help but think he's going to lose his cool about me having a guy but he doesn't. He actually looks okay about it.

"You two are a very cute couple and I really hope you enjoy the wedding," Zoe says.

I hold on to Leo's hand. "I'm sure we will."

Fake green ivy hangs from golden frames around the room and white material covers the walls and the seats. This room is even more stunning than the honeymoon suite and the reception area. I spot Leo sitting on the third row.

"I've got to admit they've really pulled out all the stops. It looks great doesn't it?" Bria whispers to me.

The church is full, even though there are several empty seats on Dad's side. It was nicer than I thought seeing family members as they arrived. The only thing that annoyed me was Aunty Nora, my dad's sister, who was asking after my mum. I wish she'd had that same concern when Mum turned to her for help.

"It looks lovely," I respond.

Two of Zoe's best friends, Rebecca and Mindy, are the other bridesmaids and they're talking in hushed voices. I suddenly realise that I'm the only bridesmaid from Dad's side of the family.

"Oh my goodness," gasps Rebecca. "You look beautiful!"

I turn to see who she's talking to. And there she is. Zoe walks towards us like a heavenly vision in a white floaty dress that fits her bump perfectly. She's holding a bouquet of white roses and wild lavender in her hand. She looks beautiful.

"You all look amazing!" She looks at us all one by one. "Let's do this!"

We form two rows in front of Zoe, first me and Bria, and then Mindy and Rebecca. We all seem to take a deep breath at the same time and suddenly the nerves come back, but this time it's not just me. We fall silent as the music starts and everybody in the church rises and turns to look at the back of the room. I hear the gasps and coos as we begin to walk.

Dad and his Best Man, an uncle I don't know well, stands at the front of the room. Dad shuffles nervously from foot to foot and his eyes light up when he sees Zoe.

I can feel Leo watching me as I walk. I catch his eye and I wink at him.

He mouths, "Beautiful."

The lights are low and everybody is sat in the dining room for the reception. The ceremony was simple and gorgeous and I'm stuffed from the five course meal.

Leo makes his way over to the bar to grab us both a drink before we go. Dad and Zoe are walking around thanking everyone for coming. Dad spots me and whispers something to Zoe before hurrying over.

"So, what did you think?"

"It was amazing." And it was.

"I'm so glad you're here, baby," Dad says.

"I am too Dad."

Leo makes his way back from the bar and hands me a drink.

"Congratulations Mr Brown, it was a beautiful day," Leo says.

"Thank you and thanks for looking after my Marni for me." He pats Leo on the shoulder.

"My pleasure, sir."

"We're going to get a move on Dad," I say. "Enjoy the rest of your night."

Dad kisses me on the forehead before he makes his way to Zoe and her friends who are dancing and screaming out the words to a Whitney song. I watch Dad walk away and I hope that this is the beginning of something new for all of us.

"Glad you came?" Leo asks as we put on our coats.

I nod. "I'm happy. I haven't felt this good in a long time."

"You deserve it," Leo says.

We leave the dining hall and walk down the corridor. For the first time in years everything feels just right. My parents are getting the help they both need, I'm closer than ever to Sanaa, I've got this amazing guy beside me and I haven't had a panic attack in a while.

I think *finally* everything is going to be okay and if I'm honest, it feels really great being Amani.

ABOUT THE AUTHOR

Annabelle Steele has been working as a primary school teacher for eight years; holding a BA in Journalism and a Postgraduate Certificate in Primary Teaching. She's been writing Young Adult and Children's fiction for over 20 years, but has only recently found the courage to share her work.

Through her writing, Annabelle explores mental health, relationships, and the realities of being part of a minority group living in the UK.

She lives in Manchester with her husband and son. When she isn't with her family or working Annabelle enjoys reading, writing and doing anything that allows her to get creative.

READING GROUP QUESTIONS

1.   How do you think you would have responded to Amani's Mum and Dad if you were Amani?

2.   How does the novel deal with the idea of guilt? In what different ways do you think Amani's parents felt guilty?

3.   Why do you think Amani's grandad is able to work with Levi to try to build a relationship with Amani despite what happened between him and his daughter? Would you be able to be as understanding?

4.   What do you think the future holds for Amani's mum? What do you want to happen to her in the future?

5.   What do you think the future holds for Amani and Leo? Do you think they are really in love?

6.   Would you have gone to the wedding if you were Amani?

7.   What do you think the future holds for Amani and Sanaa? Can their friendship last?

8.   Do you think Amani knew why Ryan was taking her upstairs at the party? Did she want to sleep with him at any point? What do you think contributed to the mental battles she was having during this scene?

9.   *"Do you ever do other styles with your hair?" I scoff, hoping*

he's joking, but as he lifts the ends of one of my braids, I see he's serious. "What do you mean?" I ask slowly. "Well, it's just always down and in these." He's furrowing his brow as he twiddles the braid between his thumb and forefinger. I want to knock it out of his hand, but I don't. What would you do in this situation? What do you think Amani should have done or said to Ryan?

10. What do you think the future is for Amani and her dad? How does this differ from what you want the future to be for them?

11. *"Tyler Baxter!" I shout and all four of the customers in front of us turn and look. I know exactly what they're thinking, 'loud, obnoxious, Black teens' but for once I don't care.* What do you think Amani means by 'for once I don't care'? What does this tell us about Amani and how she believes that the world perceives her? Do you think she has a realistic perception of her place in the world?

12. *As they pass, the children look me up and down and the women pretend not to notice me, but I see them exchange a bewildered glance when they think I'm not watching. I've never felt so Black.* How do you think Amani felt in this situation? Can you relate this to an experience of your own?